DELETED SCENES
AND OTHER BONUS FEATURES

stories by

Kevin Catalano

STEPHEN F. AUSTIN STATE UNIVERSITY PRESS

For information about permission to reproduce selections from this book, contact *permissions* :

Stephen F. Austin State University Press
P.O. Box 13007, SFA Station
Nacogdoches, TX 75962
sfapress@sfasu.edu
www.sfasu.edu/sfapress
936-468-1078

Project Manager: Kimberly Verhines
Cover Design: Jason Hopkins

ISBN: 978-1-62288-303-5

Some of these stories have appeared in various forms in (respectively) *Monkeybicycle; Cease, Cows; Gargoyle Magazine; Alternating Current Press; 100 Word Story; Denver Syntax; PANK; storySouth; People Holding; Used Furniture Review; Go Read Your Lunch; Gamut; FRiGG; Surreal South '13.*

Also by Kevin Catalano
Where the Sun Shines Out

For Mom and Dad

TABLE OF CONTENTS

THE EXISTENTIAL CRISIS OF NICOLAS CAGE
(IN HIS OWN WORDS)

What are you doing here?

Get in the car!

Which direction are we going?

Do you trust me?

There's two different kinds of trust.

One of them's me. The other's not you.

You're funny.

Let's ride!

Why are you here? What do you want from me?

I saw you and you saw me. Don't pretend you don't know who I am, girly man.

You ruined my life.

We aren't here to make things perfect. The snowflakes are perfect. The stars are perfect. Not us. Not us! We are here to ruin ourselves and to break our hearts and love the wrong people and die.

It's like we're on two different channels now.

Maybe if you drank bourbon with me, it would help. Maybe if you kissed me and I could taste the sting in your mouth it would help.

You and I share the same DNA. Is there anything more lonely than that?

I was the same man who was not good enough for you before, and I'm just not good enough for you now.

Do you ever get the feeling that there's something...powerful pressing down on you?

Maybe...maybe emotion becomes so intense your body just can't contain it. Your mind and your feelings become too powerful, and your body weeps.

The past and the future is a joke to me now. I see that they're nothing. I see they ain't here. The only thing that's here is you—and me.

If you drank bourbon with me naked. If you smelled of bourbon as you fucked me, it would help. It would increase my esteem for you.

The way your head works is God's own private mystery. I'm the guy who made a deal with the devil.

How deep is hell?

300 feet. Pretty neat, pretty neat.

If I can spend the rest of my life as a free man without a curse from Hell hanging over my head, yeah, I'll take it.

Sometimes it's a hard world for small things.

I remember once imagining what my life would be like, what I'd be like. I pictured having all these qualities, strong positive qualities that people could pick up on from across the room. But as time passed, few ever became any qualities that I actually had. And all the possibilities I faced and the sorts of people I could be, all of them got reduced every year to fewer and fewer. Until finally they got reduced to one, to who I am.

I'm sorry I let you down.

I just blurted it out, I'm sorry.

I'll tell you right now, I'm in love with you. But be that as it may, I am not here to force my twisted soul into your life.

I like you, too, but what's the point in any of it? Fuck to this day. I mean, fuck to this day. It's all just gonna boil up and wash us away. Maybe you'll still be here. Maybe you won't.

You are what you love, not what loves you. Keep going, man.

You all right?

I'm in a little trouble.

You're doing fine.

I spent last Tuesday watching fibers on my carpet. And the whole time I was watching my carpet, I was worrying that I, I might vomit. And the whole time, I was thinking, "I'm a grown man. I should know what goes on in my head." And the more I thought about it... the more I realized that I should just blow my brains out and end it all. But then I thought, well, if I thought more about blowing my brains out... I start worrying about what that was going to do to my goddamn carpet.

Have some coke on me. Pull the car over.

What?

Pull it over!

Don't you want to get high and get laid? Fuck you right now.

Cool it man!

You ruined my life!

No one said survival was fun. Just pull over.

I misbehaved. I have to be punished. But remember... Every time when you look in the mirror, you'll see my face.

[To himself] He may have my soul, but he doesn't have my spirit.

CREDITS

<u>CAST</u>
Nicolas Cage

<u>FILMS REFERENCED</u>
<u>(in alphabetical order)</u>
8mm
Adaptation City of Angels
Con Air
Face Off
Ghost Rider
Ghost Rider: Spirit of Vengeance
Gone in Sixty Seconds
It Could Happen to You
Joe
Leaving Las Vegas
Lord of War Moonstruck
National Treasure: Book of Secrets
Rage
Raising Arizona
Snake Eyes
Trapped in Paradise
The Croods
The Weather Man
Wild at Heart

GHOST IN THE WOMB

When the blood bubbled up from the shower drain of the house we just moved into, I thought: here we go. This is the beginning of it. Just like in the movies, it begins with blood, and then the flies come, the hurled furniture, the claw marks—and the couple living there will try to tough it out. One of them will scream, "This is my home!" But after the climactic scene where they barely survive, involving a torn-open hole to a ghostly dimension located in their basement, they will quickly move out.

It always begins with blood.

My wife was at work when it happened, thank god. She couldn't handle much since becoming pregnant. The other day, mounting a curtain rod, the dry wall crumbled on her head. She screamed and bent the rod over her knee and went up to the bedroom to cry. I brought her an ice cream sandwich, the only thing that settled her these days.

The blood seemed fresh, warm as the inside of a person. It had a texture to it—liquid meat, something you fist. I called a plumber.

"It's blood alright," said the plumber, an orange, old-country Italian. He'd removed the shower floor, and we both stared down into the pipe. I was uneasy about seeing such exposed things, like what's below my feet in the ocean or inside my wife's uterus.

"Where'd it come from?" I asked.

"The blood? Hell if I know. Came from this pipe, I can tell you that."

"You don't seem too surprised."

"Son, you know what I've found in people's pipes?"

Much later, I wished I'd offered guesses: a first-edition Superman comic, the 12-inch Chewbacca I never got for Christmas, human teeth.

What I did think to ask him was: Do we see things in pipes that we put there ourselves? If so, what was it that he put in people's pipes? And whose blood did I put in ours?

People who stare into shadows seeking forms should not be allowed to view an ultrasound. I tried to explain this to Sara, but for the past few weeks, her capacity for logic had disappeared. Her freckled nose would scrunch at my attempts to syllogistically break down a problem: I am afraid of ghosts; ultrasounds take ghostly pictures of babies; therefore, I am afraid of ultrasounds.

"You're stupid," was her final comment as she waited at the door, digging into her nose with her pinky, ready to be taken to the hospital.

Nurse was a beautiful black man the size of two men. He smelled of jasmine and appeared to be wearing eyeliner. He sat next to Sara laid out on the table and announced, "I'm going to squirt some warm jelly on you now." He did just as he said. Sara squirmed and giggled as the tube farted out gel. When Nurse rolled the wand over her belly, Sara doubled up and laughed. "Oh my God, it tickles so bad!"

Eventually, she settled, and Nurse proceeded. What danced on the monitor yanked at my throat and poked at my bladder, a sensation that seemed to also affect my bladder. It was like digital smoke, oozing and morphing around in liquid pitch. At one point, its head turned to reveal a face, except it was unfinished: big gaping holes for the eyes and mouth. I tried to disguise my terror, but it seeped out, first in a squeak between my pursed lips, then as tears.

Mercifully, Nurse stopped. He flicked on the lights and printed out pictures of the spirit. When he handed them to me, I couldn't hold on anymore. I pissed myself, soaking my jeans down to my thighs. Sara laughed hysterically, but Nurse was affectionate. He put his hand on my shoulder as I waddled out of the room.

"It's a beautiful day in your life," he cooed, his breath smelling of burnt coffee, but the rest of him like flowers from my childhood, the kind my mother picked from the garden on spring mornings to place on the kitchen table. I yearned for him to pick me up and hold me in his massive arms, but Sara was rummaging through the bowl of candy at the counter, scattering lollipops all over the receptionist's desk.

The blood began spitting from all the faucets. It was chunky and stank of aluminum and fruit. I noticed it when Sara was filling the coffee pot with water, her bump brushing the counter. If she noticed, she didn't care. She poured the blood into the coffee maker and filled the filter with grounds.

"Wait," I said from the couch before she turned it on. "Switch on the faucet again."

She did, and it ran frothy red. Then she turned it off. "Anything else I can do for you?" She got out a cereal bowl and poured in the Honey Nut Cheerios and two handfuls of mini marshmallows.

I was worried, less about the blood than her. She was oblivious; she would drink that water and brush her teeth with it, and if she'd do that, then what else would she do? The coming weeks would answer. She became clumsier; she began breaking dishes, dropping the canister of sugar, spilling milk on my laptop. She forgot doctor's appointments, her daily vitamins, the time. She would often forget she had to work that morning, and when I reminded her, she'd come downstairs wearing sweatpants, one of my T-shirts, and black knee-high boots.

It was a girl. I suffered through another ultrasound, this one worse. The fetus's spine glowed in the dark like one of those prehistoric fish, the kind that appear in the dark ocean of my dreams. As tears ran down my face, Nurse hugged me and said I'd be a wonderful father. Sara was singing *Gagaga- girl!* as she skipped down the hall.

That was twenty weeks in, which marked when the banging started. I was grading papers—Sara upstairs asleep snuggling up with her body pillow— when it first happened. It started as muffled thuds that a normal person would have blamed on the furnace or old plumbing. Then it was pounding, so hard the walls shook, knocking my beer onto the papers. The light fixtures rattled and the few pictures we had hung on the wall crashed. There seemed to be a pattern to it—definitely at night and after Sara had eaten. When she was active, it was quiet. Of course, this was something else Sara didn't notice, not even when we were watching TV on the couch and the pounding became so violent that a chunk of wall collapsed on my head.

Christmas break was nearing, which meant classes were almost over, and that Central NY winter was digging in its heels, the freezing wind whipping through the holes and cracks in the walls created daily by our ghost. I was frayed.

Being an academic man, home repair eluded me, but I had to learn it. Every morning and evening I was on a ladder, slathering the spackle. At rare slivers of time, when the pounding had ceased and Sara wasn't balling her eyes out at some incomprehensible problem, I felt productive and needed and masculine. My hands were blistered and cut up and caked—not the smooth, manicured hands of academia—and I had accomplished something visible; I had repaired a wall that kept the winter from my pregnant wife. The tiny dick in my pants swelled with pride.

Until the ghost thundered once more, destroying my work.

In the deepest corner of the sea, a strange creature lolls in the tar. Its body is translucent, its spine neon blue, its organs yellow balloons, its face a jellied skull. It will never be discovered by humans, though just once, in its interminable timeline stretching far beyond the extinction of man, some unlucky soul will dream its exact form.

I held Sara in my arms at 3 a.m., rocking her and humming. She had woken screaming again, her hair matted to her damp forehead despite the cold night air breathing through the unfixable holes in the roof and walls. The stars in the winter sky winked. An owl had perched just inside our bedroom, who-who--who-ing in what I believed was a logical rhythm. There were squirrels racing around our living room. A family of deer visited on occasion to rummage the refrigerator. Ants swarmed the sticky blood that seeped from the walls.

Sara was now twenty-four months pregnant.

The baby was kicking again. Sara's drumskin belly jumped and bulged. The doctor said she wasn't ready, though he never specified which *she*. But I knew. Girly wasn't ready because there was no Girl. There was no baby, or there was one once, and then there wasn't, and the difference between the was and the wasn't became its own entity, an in-between thing that will not come out. I had to find a way to deliver this half-thing and feed it to the animals. Get it out of here. This is my home.

DELETED SCENES

PLAY ALL
COMMENTARY **ON**/OFF

Drawing Snakes.

Open on Little Mary Ramy, seven years old, wearing a purple Super Friends sweatshirt. She's sitting on the kitchen floor with markers, a tablet of paper, and fantastic drawings of snakes strewn about her. The camera revolves around her while cutting in, at various times, on close-ups of the drawings—the intricate scales, tubular bodies coiled in complex shapes, the vacant eyes. Mary's mother walks in and crouches to investigate. She picks up a drawing, shakes her head, and crumples it.

"Snakes are gross, honey," she tells Mary, tossing the paper ball at her feet. "Draw something girly, like unicorns or rainbows or hearts—some cute crap like that."

Mary says—

Writer/Director: Okay, here we go. Great. I'm the writer and director, James Seymour. I'm probably not supposed to say this, but… this film didn't turn out the way I wanted it to. I know how that sounds, I know it. A film fails miserably, and the guy who made the film says it didn't turn out the way he wanted it to. Fine. But I'll admit it's my fault. The studio wanted me to trim it down from two and a half hours to an hour forty-five. There wasn't anything I could do about that, but I chose what to cut, and—shit, I mean, look at this. Why would I cut all these snake scenes from a film called Ouroboros?

I know why I did it at the time: to suggest the theme without banging the audience over the head. But now the film doesn't make any goddamn sense.

Dejected, Little Mary begins a new drawing, laboriously at first, then with enthusiasm, her pink tongue parting her lips. She finishes it and smiles. A close up of the drawing reveals a snake eating another snake in the shape of a heart. Fade out.

Come Tumbling Down.

On black, a high pitched, mechanical sound. Cut to a tattoo needle carving an intricately detailed snake into skin. The blood is dabbed, and the camera pulls out to 19-year-old Mary, pink tongue parting her crimson lips as she holds the tattoo gun on a man sporting a mullet. He's ogling her breasts. Mary catches him doing it but doesn't care.

Cut to the man standing in front of a mirror, examining the finished tattoo—a snake wrapped around his entire arm—confusion turning to anger. "What the fucking fuck?" he yells, wheeling around. "You crazy-ass bitch." Mary lights a cigarette, then picks at something underneath her black fingernails. The owner, a bulky man with tattooed flames swarming his bald head, steps in.

"What's the matter?"

"I asked for a dragon, and she gave me a snake. I'm not paying for this bullshit."

The man storms out. The owner turns to Mary. "You're done. I'm serious this time."

Mary jumps up. "Oh, come on! You're going to take his side?"

Writer/Director: More snakes. You take one out, you got to take them all out. What's coming up was left in, but what's currently in the film is this odd jump from Mary tattooing to that dude getting angry, and the viewer doesn't even know why he's angry.

Jumping Jack Films, those guys were great. I'm not going to blame them since they gave me my first shot. They liked the script; they put up the money. They were nice the whole way through. But, you know, they're just not artists. They think in dollars and cents, and I'm trying to get my vision on the screen, and—like here, coming up. I had it in the script that after the city crumbles and the snake slithers up Mary's skirt, the entire screen fades to white and holds on that whiteness for a solid minute. It would have been beautiful. It would do something to the eyes, I tried to tell them. It was thematically important, the idea of Mary getting this gift, this child, this blank canvas to write on. But the studio wouldn't let me do it.

Mary is in a bar, pleading with a well-dressed, middle-aged couple seated next to her. They are trying their best to ignore her, but Mary is drunk and gushing.

"I'm a hard worker. I'm reliable. I'll do anything… if you know anyone hiring. I'm just trying to—"

The couple shift away from Mary, and the bartender intervenes. "Quit freaking out my customers."

"Why don't you suck my dick," Mary snaps.

The bartender jabs a finger in her face, "Get the hell out of here, you loser. Go on, get."

"You go on and get."

Mary tosses the stool and flees, squishing up her face to stifle tears. Outside, it's late afternoon, and Mary stands on a hill overlooking the Syracuse skyline. She is crying hysterically. She grabs her head and screeches, causing the entire cityscape to tremble, then crumble in a massive display of carnage. The trees, sky, and clouds collapse into oblivion, leaving Mary gripping her head in a foreground of blinding, white nothingness. From this whiteness, something red is slithering toward her, something Mary doesn't notice. It's a long, wet snake, and it wraps around her calf and slithers up her jean skirt.

Writer/ Director: Just try to imagine that long, beautiful white.

Maybe from a Toilet Seat?

Mary sprawls out on a coffee-stained couch in a cramped basement apartment. Her hand dips in and out of a Captain Crunch box. She's been crying. There's a knock at the door and she shouts, "It's open!" Edgar, her soft-spoken and slightly overweight friend since elementary school, walks in looking worried.

"Hey," he says, sitting cross-legged on the floor next to her. "Everything okay?"

"I'm pregnant," Mary blurts out. "What? Who?"

"Me, that's who. I'm pregnant."

"No, I mean, who with? Who's the father?"

Mary sits up on her elbow. "That's the crazy thing... I don't know. I don't mean I don't remember. I mean... hell... I haven't gotten laid in over a year."

Edgar scratches his head. "Maybe from a toilet seat?"

"Oh, that's right," Mary says sarcastically. "Now that you mention it, I do remember getting boned by a toilet."

"Jeez, I'm just trying to help."

"I don't know what I'm going to do," Mary says, collapsing back down on the couch.

"Whatever happens," Edgar says, "I mean, whatever you decide to do, I can help you out."

Writer/Director: Now, come on. How could I cut this? How else is the audience supposed to know that Mary got pregnant without having sex? I think I was, again, trying to suggest, hoping the audience would figure out the Mary and Immaculate Conception deal. After all, it's an independent film. A thinky film. I first pitched this as the next Donnie Darko. *But what was it* Time-Out *said? 'Watching* Ouroboros *is like watching a David Lynch film when you're not high.' I guess these days people don't want to think. You got to hold their hand and show them what everything means.*

Edgar and Mary are holding hands. Edgar kisses her knuckles, and when she doesn't object to that, he moves in to awkwardly kiss her lips. Mary recoils.

"Edgar! What the eff?"

"Sorry," Edgar says, standing. "I have to go. I have...library books overdue."

As Edgar leaves, focus on a nonplussed Mary. She absently pushes her hand into the cereal box. Fade out.

The Birthmark.

Mary is sitting on her filthy couch, feeding the baby she's cradling and watching *Northern Exposure* on TV. As she holds the bottle, she gently massages the baby's chest and stomach until she notices something on her ribcage: a birthmark in the shape of a small S.

Mary examines it closer. She pulls up her shirt and contorts her head so she can see her own, identical birthmark.

At that moment, Susan, Mary's mother, comes into the apartment.

Susan is attractive for her age due to the breast implants, BoTox injections, and bright-yellow-dyed hair. She beams at the sight of her daughter and granddaughter, giving both a kiss.

"Mom," Mary says, handing over the baby, "I want you to take a close look at her."

"Have you named her yet?" Susan asks, cooing at the infant. "You have to name her. You have to name her and baptize her right away. I'm dating a priest or a reverend or some crap like that. He'll do it for you. He's so adorable."

"Mom, just look at the baby."

"Oh, how cute," Susan says. "She looks just like you." "Look at this." Mary points to the baby's birthmark. There's a knock on the door, and Mary calls, "Come in!"

Paul, Mary's dad, enters. He's a barrel-chested man wearing a tucked-in flannel and muddy work boots. The moment he sees Susan, he says, "What is this? You didn't tell me she'd be here."

"Oh, get over it, Paul," Susan says.

"Dad, this is important. Come here, and look at the baby."

Writer/Director: I was in awe directing John and Renee, not to mention Vanessa, of course. Vanessa was fantastic, but there was some push-back from John and Renee. I had this funny feeling the whole time that they didn't trust me. I was the new director who made a few commercials and that Bjork video; otherwise, nobody knew who I was. So I had to prove myself. In that scene especially, I thought they were playing it a little campy, and I told them the humor would come through more if they played it straight. But, you know, it's John Charles and Renee Foyer. You can't really tell them how to act, so I quit trying. I guess it doesn't matter anyway since it was all cut. This part coming up—this stayed in.

Mary with baby unlocks the front door of the tattoo parlor. The bright sun coming through the windows shows it's early morning. Mary calls out into the shop just to be sure she's alone. She walks over to her station, takes out a clean needle from its package, and inserts it into the gun. Then she grabs the ink.

"Listen," she says to the baby, who looks back at her earnestly. "I'm so very sorry, but this is going to hurt a little. But it will tell us what we need to know...I think."

Mary looks at the baby and exhales, then lifts the blanket from its chubby leg, turns on the gun, and quickly pricks her with it, just above the knee. The baby cries. Mary repeats, "I'm so sorry." Mary holds the baby to her chest, exhales, then pulls up her skirt to look at her own knee. There, a faint but unmistakable bluish dot. She rubs at it just to be sure. It is permanent. Cut to black.

Mr. Brimmer.

On black, the sounds of an audience echo in an expansive room. Fade in to a wide shot of people of assorted professions—teachers, bankers, a police officer, etc.—seated in a high school auditorium. Mary's parents are sitting in the front row with Edgar between them.

Writer/Director: Aw, man. I'm going to be sick watching this. My brother, Kenny, plays Mr. Brimmer, the funniest part of this whole scene, and I just had to hack it out. Kenny's still not talking to me about that. Since we were kids, it was our dream that I would make films and he would act in them. It seemed like we'd made it, and then I had to call him up at the chicken processing plant and tell him I cut him from the picture. I remember he argued with me about it, told me to stand my ground. I didn't and, of course, he was right.

Mary walks onto the stage carrying Little Mary, who is now about eight months old, more personality on her dimpled, smiling face. Mary puts the baby into a high chair on the stage, and then she looks around the room and calls out, "Can I get everyone's attention, please?"

Everyone shushes, and Mary begins.

"Thank you all for coming on such short notice. I'm sure you're wondering why I asked you all to be here, so I'll get right to it. This baby"— cut to Little Mary clumsily putting Captain Crunch into her mouth—"is me. It's been proven and verified. I don't know why or how, but that's just how it is. Now, I'm sure all of you can vouch for the fact that I'm a screw up."

Cut to the audience vehemently agreeing.

"I'm broke, I'm a neurotic mess, I have no education, no love life to speak of, and now, I'm a single mother on welfare. The reason you all are here is that each of you played a part in screwing up my life. Mrs. Selton is here, my first grade teacher, who failed me for coloring outside the lines. Hi, Mrs. Selton."

Mrs. Selton waves cheerily, happy to be there.

"There's Jimmy Meyers, who made up that rumor in the 9th grade that I got a frozen hotdog stuck up in me and had to have surgery to get it out."

Jimmy Meyers, now a police officer, pumps his fist proudly.

"And, of course, my parents, who couldn't have done a worse job raising me." Susan and Paul wink at each other.

"And the list goes on. The good news is, however, that we were all given a second chance when I gave birth to myself. What I am asking from each of you is to help me raise Little Mary here better than I was raised by reenacting all of the important moments of my childhood, except we're going to spin them to have a positive outcome."

There is murmuring from the audience. Here, Mary points to a table just below the stage stacked with thick, white booklets. She leans down to Edgar and her parents and says something. They stand and begin handing out booklets to everyone in the auditorium.

"What you are being given is a script that dramatizes every pivotal moment from my life. You all will be reenacting these moments for Little Mary here, in the hopes that the damages will be undone and I—she will have a better future. Of course, some of you won't be needed for a while, not until Mary is the right age."

Writer/Director: Here he comes. I can't watch.

"For example, Mr. Brimmer, my 10th grade gym teacher who molested me in his office and then told me I would grow up fat and never amount to anything…we won't need you for another thirteen years or so."

Mr. Brimmer is reading his part in the script, then raises his hand. "Says here that I still molest you, but afterwards, I tell you that you will grow up to be President?"

"That's right. Is there a problem with that?"

"No, it just seems like maybe I shouldn't molest you at all." The audience murmurs in agreement. Other hands shoot up.

"Look, when you all get pregnant and have yourself as a child, then you can write your own goddamn script." Little Mary begins to squirm in her seat, and Mary gets more Captain Crunch from her diaper bag and puts it on the tray. After popping some cereal into her own mouth, she continues, "Fact is, Mr. Brimmer, I kind of liked having sex with you."

Mr. Brimmer shrugs, "Oh, okay." "So, what everyone needs to do is—"

Writer/Director: I'm sorry, Kenny.

It Was Because of You.

A series of dissolving shots show Mary with script in hand directing various groups of people, with Little Mary as the focus. First, Little Mary is being pushed on a swing by "her" father, Mary making sure he is in the right place this time so he catches her fall backwards. Second, Little Mary is slightly older, in first grade, and Mrs. Selton tells her that her coloring is beautiful. Third—

Writer/Director: A montage. Such an overused technique; I tried so hard to avoid it. I used to have this fantasy that when people would look back at my body of work, some film-school nerd writing his dissertation would notice that I never once used a montage. And here I am watching this shitty technique. I just couldn't figure out a better way to get that information across. Maybe there's a better filmmaker out there who could have figured it out. The hell of it is, it wasn't even the montage that was cut but this scene coming up.

The sequence moves out of its montage to a wide shot in the kitchen of Mary's childhood home. Little Mary, now 8 years old, sits at the dinner table with Susan and Paul as they go through their lines.

Paul, obviously acting, says mechanically to Susan, "I am willing to forgive your indiscretion, but I would like to know what you saw in him."

"That you didn't see in me," Mary whispers, following along with the script. "That you didn't see in me," Paul says.

Susan replies, doing slightly better with the acting, "He paid attention to me. That's all it was, and that's all I needed." Suddenly, Susan breaks from character and says to Mary, "I'm sorry, I can't do this."

"What's wrong?"

"This isn't why we got divorced, Mary." "Susan," Paul warns.

Little Mary says to Susan, "What's going on, Mommy?"

Mary says to Edgar who is standing with her, "Will you take Mary into the next room for a minute?"

Edgar lifts Little Mary up, blowing a fart on her stomach as he carries her. She giggles.

When they are gone, Mary says, "What the hell is going on? You can't break character in front of Mary like that."

"I can't lie about this anymore," Susan says. "Your father and I didn't get divorced because I cheated on him. We got divorced because of you."

Mary is shocked and looks at Paul for confirmation. "It's true," he says. "You demanded so much attention that we had no time for each other. Apparently, it happens to a lot of couples."

"We're sorry we didn't tell you before," Susan says. "We didn't want to hurt your feelings."

"Hurt my feelings! JesuseffingChrist." Mary stares out the window for a beat—

Cut to black.

Drawing Snakes Revisited.

Open on Little Mary wearing a yellow Powerpuff Girls sweatshirt, sitting on the floor of the dirty apartment with markers, a tablet of paper, and fantastic drawings of snakes strewn about her. The camera revolves around her while cutting in on the close-ups of the snakes' faces.

Writer/Director: Since I cut the first scene, it didn't make sense to keep this. Funny, watching all these deleted scenes together, it almost tells its own little story. I think that makes it worse.

Mary walks into the room, sees the drawings, and gets upset. "No no no no no," she says, picking up all of the drawings and crumpling them up. "You can't draw snakes. You can't."

"Why not?"

"Because you just can't. Draw unicorns or something." Mary suddenly hears what she says. "I mean, just don't draw anything. You can't draw. You're not very good at it. Why don't we put a puzzle together? Would you like that?"

Close in on Little Mary, confused and sad. Cut to black.

Christmas, Unscripted.

Fade in to the Shoppingtown Mall adorned with Christmas decorations. Little Mary, Paul, and Susan are standing in a long line waiting to see Santa.

Edgar and Mary are standing off to the side. Mary is making a note in the script.

Writer/Director: You'll notice at the end of this sequence that I was allowed to shoot my white-screen idea. Of course, it didn't make it in. I was saying earlier that it plays a trick on the eye. I did this once in a short I made in film school. When you look at a white screen for more than 30 seconds, you begin to fill it in with your own images. It's a strange phenomenon, as if the eye isn't comfortable with blankness. The idea is that the viewer would be the director in these small segments, participating in the visuals. In a film about a woman who isn't satisfied with the way her life went and who gets the opportunity to recreate it, I thought it important that the audience also get the opportunity to recreate their vision of the film. But try explaining this to someone who only thinks about the bottom line. It's like explaining Bergman to a baby.

"I'm just curious to know if any of this is helping, that's all," Edgar says.
"Well, I feel better," Mary says. "I feel better about myself, and I don't
    think I'm allergic to cats anymore."
"I don't see how what you're doing with your daughter would change what you're allergic to."
"She's not my daughter, Edgar. She's me. There's a huge difference."
"She *is* your daughter. And I'm worried that you're screwing her up more
    than helping her."
"Helping me, you mean."
"Listen," Edgar says, putting his hand on Mary's arm. "What you're doing is just…odd. I mean, look at all this." The camera pans to shoppers in the mall, all of whom have scripts. Close up of Santa, reading from his script to a child, who is also reading from a script. "This is not normal. This is not even close to normal."
Mary jerks her arm from Edgar. She is clearly upset. "I'm just trying to have a good effing life for once!" As she turns to leave, she collides with a man holding a tray of Orange Juliuses, drenching Mary. She screams, "That wasn't in the script!" then runs off.
Cut to Mary driving her car recklessly, tears and sticky juice streaming down her face. She pounds the steering wheel, swerving in and out of lanes. The stereo blasts harsh, electronic music. Suddenly, a sixteen-wheeler is heading right for her, its horn blaring. The truck collides with her car. Shards

from the windshield explode, and then a flash of white light holds on the screen for a long moment. Cut to black.

Losing Virginity, Again.

Cut in to Paul, Susan, Edgar, and "Little" Mary (no longer little at 12) all dressed in black and standing in a cemetery as a casket is lowered into the ground. This shot dissolves into the next, where Paul and Susan, with scripts in hand, are directing a group of girls and Mary on the school playground. Edgar looks on disapprovingly. The older girls are smoking cigarettes, and when they offer one to Mary, she refuses. When the scene is over, and Paul and Susan aren't looking, Mary snatches a cigarette from the girl and puffs on it. This dissolves into another scene with Paul and Susan at the helm, and Mary, now 15—

Writer/Director: Oh, right. As if one montage isn't enough. What was cut here is the only sex scene in the film. The studio wanted this to be PG-13 to attract a wider audience. This, after begging Vanessa to get naked for the camera. I think she regretted doing it and never quite forgave me for persuading her. She's such an attractive, funny, smart girl. I had this fantasy that she would maybe fall for me during the shooting, but I blew that. Let's be honest, I'm not an attractive guy, but I thought maybe Vanessa would be attracted to talent or whatever. [Off microphone, barely audible] Um... can we cut that last part?

The montage ends at a large pick-up truck in a secluded gravel lot in a wooded park. Susan and Paul are once again in charge of the scene. Mary, now 16, is in the bed of the truck making out with Owen, a 35 year-old man. Pillows and blankets are laid out. Candles have been set up on the sides, while a Justin Timberlake track plays from the truck's radio.

Mary lies on her back, and Owen unzips his jeans. Cut to Paul and Susan scrutinizing each movement. Paul half-whispers to Owen, "You have condoms, right?" Owen nods. "Put two on," Paul says.

Owen does, and Susan directs, "Now, nice and sweet, just like we talked about. Nice and romantic." Owen enters Mary, then proceeds to gently make love to her. Mary yawns.

After a minute of this, Mary pushes him off. "This is awful. If this is my first time, I want it to be good!" She turns, gets on her hands and knees, and looks over her shoulder at Owen. "Now give it to me, dammit."

Owen looks at Susan and Paul.

Paul tells Mary, "This is supposed to be a romantic memory."

"Screw that. Now come on asshole," she yells at Owen, who shrugs and kneels behind her.

Cut to Paul and Susan wide-eyed as the noises get loud and graphic. They turn and walk slowly away.

Return to the Tattoo Parlor.

Writer/Director: How many more of these scenes are there? This is torture.

Cut to Mary walking into a tattoo parlor with a notebook of sketches. We see Mary through the window talking to a bald, heavily tattooed man, showing him her drawings. He explains something to her and shakes her hand.

Cut to Mary in a crummy apartment, sitting on the couch in the dark, wearing a puffy coat, hat, and scarf, as she eats a milkless bowl of Captain Crunch for dinner.

Cut to Mary tattooing a man with her tongue peaking from her lips. The man is staring at her breasts, but Mary doesn't care. He examines his tattoo in the mirror, a snake that extends the length of his arm, and says, "What the fucking fuck?"

Cut to Mary pleading with a nice, middle-aged couple in a bar. The bartender kicks her out.

Cut to Mary screaming outside, the skyline, the sky, everything crumbling into white nothingness, and then a long, red snake slithers up her leg, into her skirt. Mary moans.

Cut to Mary's pregnant stomach. Cut to Edgar.

Cut to black.

Alternate Ending – Edgar's Second First Kiss.

On black, there's a knock at the door. Mary's voice says, "Come in!" Open on Edgar walking into the filthy apartment. Mary sprawls on the coffee-stained couch, her hands on her pregnant belly. She is watching *Iron Chef*, squinting her eyes at how good the food looks.

"Edgar, what are you doing here?" "I came to talk, if that's okay."
"My mom and dad didn't send you, did they?"

"No, I just came by to see how you are." Edgar kicks some empty Captain Crunch boxes clear from the floor and sits down.

Mary gives him a look that says everything: she's horrible, she's confused, she could die.

Edgar exhales. "You don't know who the father is, do you?" Mary sits up on her elbow. "How the hell do you know that?"

"There's something you should know, Mary. It's about your...baby. It's about your real mother. I'm sorry I didn't tell you."

Writer/Director: You know what I'm going to do? I'm going to do a Director's Cut. That way, everyone can see how I intended this film to look. All of these deleted scenes would be included. Maybe I'll even reshoot a few things. I'll figure out how to pass time without a goddamn montage. Maybe Kenny could play Edgar. He could pull it off. No, that wouldn't work. He's good as Mr. Brimmer, and Seth wouldn't be too happy if I just took him out of the film. Still, I could do it. The film's all there. I could re-cut it, and we could repackage the thing and okay, maybe they couldn't re-release it in theaters, but on DVD. Sure, they could do that. And then, on the comments feature, I wouldn't be sitting there like an asshole forced to talk about how I fucked up. Because this really is a good film, and if people got the chance to see what I meant to—

COMMENTARY ON/**OFF**

Mary says, "So this baby...could be me?" "I know it sounds crazy, but yes."

Mary looks down at her stomach, then she lifts her shirt to the S birthmark, elongated from her swollen belly. Edgar puts his hand on Mary's wrist.

"There's something else," Edgar says. "Something I want to ask you. I want you to think very hard about it."

"Okay."

"Do you remember that I was your first kiss? It was at the back of the bus, second grade. You were wearing a purple Super Friends sweatshirt and white spandex. You had just taken a bite of a tuna fish sandwich that you didn't eat at lunch, and then you gave me a bite of it. It was warm and disgusting. You threw the rest of it out the bus window. You wiped some mayonnaise from my mouth, then put up a Trapper Keeper to shield us from all the other kids... and then you kissed me. Do you remember that?"

Mary is staring vacantly at the TV. "That sounds vaguely familiar."

Edgar stands from the floor and sits next to her on the edge of the couch. "You've cut the good memories out. You only focused on the bad ones. Believe me, there were bad ones. But that day on the bus, kissing you, for me, that was one of the best days. I am better for it, and I was wondering if you...if you were better for it?"

"I know that—at least it seems like—I've known you longer than my life." Mary touches Edgar's fingernails, inches up to his knuckles. She asks his hand, "Will you help me remember that day?"

"Like I said, you were wearing that sweatshirt—"

"No, Edgar," Mary says, holding his hand now, eyes wide. "Will you help me *remember*?"

Edgar's face softens, and he leans into her. He smiles and whispers, "We need a Trapper Keeper."

Mary laughs, grabs his face, and kisses him. A flash of white light fills the screen. It holds for a long moment, wherein Mary and Edgars' forms seem to eventually revive.

Cut to black.

AN AMERICAN SEEKER

Heidi returned from her job at the Watchung Bank and Loan that evening, and she was glad to find that Paul had already left for work. For the first time in their four-year relationship, Heidi began snooping through Paul's things. The cargo shorts Paul had worn while tending bar were balled up on the carpet next to his side of the bed. They were dank with alcohol and sweat. She turned the pockets inside-out, and wads of cash fell to the floor along with receipts and business cards. Heidi sat cross-legged and sifted through the evidence, heart racing with expectation. The business cards were not at all interesting (mainly because they belonged to men). However, the receipts had suspicious things written on them. Many had phone numbers and email addresses, though no names. One had drawings of stick figures with stick dicks going into stick vaginas, and another, the one that really got Heidi's attention, had the words *American Psycho* written in a female's bubbly script with a heart next to it. This receipt she held onto.

Since last night, Heidi was disturbed that Paul had managed to surprise her with the marriage proposal. They were at the same semi-authentic Italian restaurant they always went to on Sunday nights, and three different waitresses delivered three different, ever-since-the-day-I-met-you lines, all of which concluded with big Paul, wincing on a knee, displaying a ring.

Heidi thought she knew him well enough to tell when he was keeping something from her. In fact, he no longer attempted to surprise her with Christmas or birthday gifts. Now, he simply asked what she wanted because she'd find the receipt for the gift, or the gift itself stupidly hidden in places he never frequented, which were the exact places she always did: the top of the coat closet where the iron was kept, under the kitchen sink with the glass cleaner and dishwasher detergent, or inside the washing machine, for Christ's sake. Heidi didn't like the version of herself that knew more about Paul than Paul did. She hated being *that* kind of woman, the type depicted in sitcoms and women's magazines—the ones who nag their dopey husbands. If dopey Paul was capable of secretly planning such an elaborate proposal, he could be capable of any other imaginable sneakiness.

She knew the night would conclude with a seat at the kitchen table, well into her third glass of pinot noir, Paul's open laptop, and looking through his emails. He didn't subscribe to social media—no Facebook or Instagram accounts. Like his clothes, his taste in music and comedies, and his relationship with technology, he was stuck in the late nineties. She used to find this endearing, until just about now, logging into his Hotmail account, typing in the same password he used for everything: *Paul123*.

Two thousand unread emails. She instinctively wanted to organize his messages, delete the obvious junk emails, and create folders for the others. She was on a mission, searching for messages from girls. Maybe *American Psycho* was a codeword he used when emailing some lonely housewife for a late-night hook-up. She did a quick Google search and discovered *American Psycho* was a novel, which only intrigued her more, since Paul wasn't a reader. She then typed the phrase into the email's search bar, but came up with nothing. She scrolled through pages and pages of messages, clicking on the ones from females whose names were unfamiliar.

A few got her attention. One from last year read: "Hope to see you this weekend" to which he had replied, "Right on"—a phrase he unfortunately overused. Mostly, these messages were harmless, though she wouldn't allow herself to quit until she had exhausted her search. She kept telling herself *one more page*, and then it was one o'clock in the morning.

She felt disgusting. Her legs were cramped from sitting in the chair at the kitchen table. The entire apartment was dark except for the blue light of the laptop screen. She groaned and got up to pee, avoiding herself in the bathroom mirror. The same impulse that compelled her to snoop, however, forced her to examine her reflection. Closely. She forced a smile, then let it go limp and studied the lines left behind. So close the mirror fogged, she held her breath and noted her freckles turning to the splotches her mother now had on her face and hands. Heidi stared hard at herself, a ruthless showdown.

She shut the lights, darkness crawling over her skin.

She muttered, "Fuck you, you old, worthless bitch."

Here was the plan: when Paul woke up tomorrow, Heidi would be reading *American Psycho* on the couch so that when he came out of the bedroom, she and the book would be the first thing he saw. Over the top of the pages, she'd carefully watch for his expression, that which would give him away. Once trapped, she'd pounce—interrogating him until he confessed his infidelity. She would have to prepare for what he might reveal: an affair that had gone on for years, perhaps with not only one woman but countless female customers—hundreds maybe. Perhaps he never worked at the bar; maybe that was a cover for cheating and he was even savvier than she recently thought. She had to be ready for anything.

There was nothing on TV that night—nothing else to do other than read the book. She hadn't planned on reading it; the book was a prop. She wouldn't admit this to most people, but her reading material of choice centered around vampires, sorcery, and King Arthur books. They didn't write these novels fast enough. She knew very well that these were what thirteen-year-old girls read, that they were considered lowbrow and so forth. But she wasn't looking to challenge her intellect or broaden her horizons, especially when she was trying to unwind and escape. She was just looking for a good read, and maybe if these literary authors got off their high horses and wrote something interesting for a change, she'd give them a try.

Heidi put on her soft, froggy pajamas, poured herself some wine, got under a blanket on the couch, and opened this novel with the horrible name. At first, she didn't get it. There was this egotistical guy who apparently loved face and hair products, who loved to exercise and listen to '80s music, and who hung out with Wall Street friends who were shallow and racist and talked about nothing other than getting reservations at fancy restaurants. Where was the psycho stuff? Heidi kept looking at the book cover to make sure she had the right one. This is so stupid, she thought, but she found it rather easy to read—not a lot of big words or fancy writing. She was over a hundred pages in when the guy narrating the book, Patrick, sliced open a homeless man's eyeball, and it ran down his face like an egg yolk. Then Patrick cut open the man's nose, and the most awful part was that he didn't kill the man; he just left him agonizing on the street with his eye cut out and his nose flayed. "Jesus," Heidi said to the book, heart throbbing in her ears. What surprised

Heidi, scared her a little, was that she began to read faster, seeking out the next violent scene.

The violence to come was unimaginable horror, and she read voraciously. This Patrick would lure various women into his extravagant Manhattan apartment and do unspeakable things to them with mace, a nail gun, a rusty coat hanger, a power drill, and—oh, Lord—what he did to one with a rat. Reading these scenes—described so carefully, in such gruesome detail—made Heidi afraid of herself. The author's trick, if it was one, was that what preceded the violence were detailed, pornographic sex scenes, so that Heidi constantly found her hand between her legs. Then, out would come the nail gun! She was convinced she was diseased in the head, the furious way she was devouring the pages, reading (hoping?) for how the author would top the previous scene's gruesomeness.

The handle of the front door jiggled. Heidi froze. It was 3 a.m. Thank God it was only Paul. She remembered the book, the plan—this could all backfire if he found her on the couch waiting up for him.

Paul opened the door, and Heidi hid the book under the blanket. He looked at her, confused, and he smiled. "Hey, baby. What are you doing up?" "Nothing," was all she managed. She noticed that the TV was off, the apartment was dark, and there was no type of reading material in sight. She must have looked creepy.

"Nothing?" he stumbled towards her, a little tipsy. He sat down next to her, unloading wads of cash onto the coffee table. "What do you mean, nothing? What were you doing?"

It was late. She was suddenly tired and irritated that she was in this position. "Just nothing, Paul," she snapped. "Leave me alone."

His big, flush face retained the smile, and now the sweet scent of liquor wafted from his mouth. "You've been acting really weird lately," he said. "Ever since I proposed to you."

Heidi bunched up the blanket to conceal the book and waddled to the bedroom. She was aware and ashamed of her behavior, but she couldn't help it. Paul followed her into the room.

"If you don't want to get married," he said, "we don't have to. We'll just go back to how it was before."

She climbed into bed, still holding the balled-up blanket. "How it was before," she repeated absently.

The hard spine of the novel had found its way between her legs. She shifted her butt to escape it, but it only pressed into her, prickling her thighs with goosebumps.

Then Paul said, "What are you hiding?" She shook her head.

"Under the blanket. I'm not an idiot."

The book rubbed at her clitoris. She bit her lip, squinted her eyes.

Paul stood still, watching her for a moment. "You're losing it," he said, and left the room.

Heidi slithered under the covers and squeezed her eyes shut. The violent images from the novel were waiting for her. One scene in particular described Patrick skinning a woman alive. Heidi felt that about herself, that someone was yanking her skin off her flesh in one long peel, revealing the purple meat underneath.

Paul had slept on the couch that night, which he often did; this time, though, he was sending her a message. So as not to wake him, she snuck out of the bedroom and through the kitchen glowing with new sun. She went into the bathroom and sat on the toilet. Her head buzzed, hung over from the late night and her gruesome dreams.

She turned on the shower and studied herself in the mirror. There, on the split of her nose, a cold sore was blossoming. It was in its pre-pus stage, bubbling the skin. Of course she would get one—it was her punishment for her behavior. She always understood her cold sores to be what kept her vanity in check. This morning, however, she surprised herself. She pulled the tip of her nose up oink-style and studied the viral skin—the pinks and reds, the tumor-like texture that deformed her. While before she would want to hide under a rock for the week, today she couldn't wait for the ooze, the gold-flaked crust of dried pus. Her own distinct, localized horror show.

Instead of going to work, she drove to the mall. She weaved in and out of the elderly mall-walkers and teenagers and stopped at a mannequin in the window of one of those boutiques that sells slutty, urban-youth apparel. The mannequin sported a fabulous black dress with a low v-neck top and a dangerously short skirt. She wore knee-high black fuck-me boots, and to top it off, a raven black, femme fatale wig. She'd walked by this display countless times in the past few weeks, always intrigued, but never sure why.

"Patricia," Heidi said, fogging the glass.

She charged into the store and ordered the sixteen-year-old texting on her phone to retrieve the dress and boots. The girl was exasperated and moved too slowly, so Heidi stepped into the showcase window and stripped the mannequin. She shimmied out of her clothes, putting on a show for the group of high-school guys who stopped to gawk. She performed a catwalk twirl before pulling on the black dress; she stepped into the boots, zipped them up her calf with slow seduction; and after positioning the wig on her head, she cocked her hip and blew a kiss at the guys—who hooted and took pictures of her on their phones—then she turned and marched out of the window.

"Hey, you can't do that," the teenager called. "It's already done."

As she strutted through the mall toward the exit, Heidi felt that the blood pumping through her had electrified, sending continuous spasms up and down her legs. She got into her car, deciding right at that moment that she—or rather, Patricia—was going to pay Paul a visit at the bar.

As she drove, she thought of the times—at least twice a year—when she would get so fed up with Paul's messiness and overall lack of drive that she'd blow up at him and demand that he make an attempt to change. For a solid week, he'd clean up his hairs from the bathroom sink, put his dishes away, and make the bed. Once, he even typed up a resume, but the only jobs it listed were at Staples and the same bar he'd been tending ever since they met, which was at the bank. At that time, she was a lowly teller, and every couple weeks he'd deposit startling wads of cash. There was plenty of time to chat as she counted the filthy bills—organizing them into sequential piles—that amounted to six-to-eight hundred dollars. She would think about his mysterious profession at night while she was in bed: a drug dealer, a ruthless bookie, a pool-playing hustler. In each scenario, she would be his fabulous accountant. This was his allure, and so she had allowed him to take her out to dinner where she couldn't wait to ask what he did for a living. Her disappointment was profound when he told her he tended bar, but as the meal progressed, she found herself charmed by his humor and affability. Even if he wasn't New Jersey's leading supplier of marijuana, there was still something enigmatic about Paul that kept her interested. Perhaps, she now thought, it was his inability to change—he remained the same old Paul despite his context. Maybe it was the fact that nobody was capable of change and, therefore, Paul was just like everybody else.

Heidi squealed into the parking lot of the bar. She looked at herself in the rearview and adjusted the black wig. Her cold sore was oozing, an orange, candy-like bubble. As Heidi stepped out of the car, she wondered whether she was evidence that people change. She charged towards the entrance with supermodel confidence—wagging her ass and swinging her arms, heals clapping the asphalt like nail-gun fire. This was not change, she thought. This was finding herself.

Heidi flung open the door and swaggered inside. She wanted to see if Paul was into the dangerous types; he might have to marry one.

A DOG NAMED SCHRÖDINGER

You are standing in front of a box. Before you go rushing off to meet your girlfriends for chocolate martinis or whatever, there's something I want to tell you about what's inside. No, I'm not playing games. *No*, I'm not stoned. Please, just hear me out for a couple of minutes because looking in the box will determine the fate of what's cramped inside.

The story of the box begins with a dog—yes, *that* dog. I found it dying in the road when I was fleeing you. Do you remember? It was about a month ago, and you had just told me—after only a year of marriage—that you didn't love me anymore. This lovely nugget of knowledge you imparted between mouthfuls of low-cal cereal while getting ready for your corporate job you're so damned pleased about. But that wasn't all you spluttered standing over the bed at God-knows what time in the morning. "I don't love you anymore, George [munch munch], but I want a baby."

So I was fleeing. I got in my shitty car and raced through the neighborhood, intent on getting the hell away from our new house your daddy bought out of town, out of the state, wherever. I got no farther than a few blocks when I came across something golden heaped by the curb, beautiful in the morning sun. I stopped and approached, saw it was a dog, and got on my knees to see its face. It looked at me with big, watery brown eyes. Then it licked my nose. That simple look and gesture was the most love I had received since before you and I were married. The sun was on our backs, my nose brushing this dog's, and my heart was flooded. I had to save its life.

I loaded it into the backseat and drove to the animal hospital. The vet, a depressingly handsome dude about my age, said this dog wasn't hit by a car, as I thought, but was just old and should probably be put down.

"By the way," Doc said, "who the hell are you?" "The owner."

"Bullshit. I know this dog. Its name is Schrödinger. And I know the owner, Dr. Copenhagen, a physics professor at Drew."

I came clean. "Dr. Copenhandler just died in a car accident—"

"Copenhagen."

"Right. With his dying breath he put me in charge of Schroder."

"Schrödinger."

"Right."

Doc wasn't amused, but after petting the dog and pondering its wagging tail he said, "I've never seen old Schrödinger so happy. Go ahead and take him. He doesn't have much time, but he's happy, and a dog should be happy at least once in his life."

Amen, Doc.

I brought the dog home and, as we both know, you weren't very happy about it. While I wanted you to be upset, in retrospect, maybe I was a bit of an asshole when I showered Schrödinger with affection in front of you and then made a special dinner for two of sausage links and ribeye steaks (what I assumed from comic strips that dogs ate) and set the dining room table with candles and our wedding china.

I was angry, okay? I polished off the remaining bottles of our "special wedding wine" and fed Schrödinger the last piece of our frozen wedding cake. Then we went to bed. That's when the fucked-up thing happened—even you have to admit that. Schrödinger had been sleeping beside me, but it certainly wasn't he who woke me in the night whispering the raunchy things from our college days, reaching into my boxers and tugging. It was a goddamn trick, working me up when I was half asleep, half drunk. I remember seeing Schrödinger in the haze, watching us intently, head cocked. Then your pale ass was waving in the half-light; you were on all fours saying, "Do me like a dog." Were you howling, too?

The next morning, it was only Schrödinger and me, along with a hangover and (what I thought were) the remnants of a wet dream. I made coffee and microwaved Hot Pockets for both of us. With nothing else to do (it was Sunday, mind you, so I didn't have to work), I sat down at the computer and searched Google for 'Schrödinger,' curious about the dog's exotic name. I clicked on the first result, and a cat flashed on the screen under the heading 'Schrödinger's Cat,' at which Schrödinger, the dog, growled. I read the page. What I discovered explains the presence of the box that's (hopefully still) in front of you. This is the important part—it's fascinating and confusing, and I don't quite understand all of it myself. I'll try to explain it the best I can. In 1935, a physicist named Erwin Schrödinger came up with a thought experiment to illustrate a paradox with quantum mechanics. This thought experiment is called Schrödinger's cat, which involves a cat in a box along with a flask of poison, some tiny bit of radioactive material, and a Geiger counter (whatever that is) that detects radioactive particles. After one hour, if the Geiger- counter thing detects the decay of a single atom from the radioactive stuff, a trigger is released and the flask is smashed, releasing the poison and killing the cat. If no decay is detected, the flask isn't crushed, and the cat remains alive.

Seems simple, right? Wrong. Because there is an equal probability that there is radioactive decay and there is no radioactive decay, and the two probabilities overlap. What this means, and hold on to your shit, is that inside the box, before anyone looks inside to see the outcome of the experiment, the cat is both alive *and* dead. What do you suppose determines the life or death of our cute little cat? You! Not until someone looks inside the box do the two realities collapse into one, at which time we'll know if we need to fetch a bowl of milk or dig a kitty grave. Reality is suspended inside the stuffy cardboard space until someone cares enough to pay attention to what's inside. If you don't appreciate the gravity of this, then all hope is lost.

It was a week later that all hope was almost lost.

I was lying out in the backyard with a cooler of beer, a bag of weed, and my new best friend, taking in the June sun (it was my day off from work, get off my back) when reality got complicated again. You came home on your lunch break to profess, "I'm pregnant and we're keeping it, so you need to find a job," and then you disappeared. As if governed by a cruel inverse proportion, the announcement of life triggered Schrödinger's preparation for death as he suddenly leveled his watery eyes on me, whimpered, then rested his head on the grass.

I was left fluttering in a fog of in-betweens—not only amidst Schrödinger's impending death and the nascent life within you, but many in-betweens that I'd apparently been existing in for a long time. I was desperate for clarity, and that's when I had the idea: *Let's make this thought experiment real.* I rummaged the neighborhood trash and found a giant refrigerator box, crawled into it with Schrödinger, and waited for you.

That's where I am now – inside this box in front of you. I don't have any fancy Geiger counter or a piece of radioactive material in here. What I do have is a bottle of rat poison, and there's a 50/50 chance I'll eat it.

I am currently in-between states, and you, the observer—my wife—are the one who will determine my reality. And who knows? Maybe this will help your own skewed perspective. Maybe it will make you look at me a little closer, choose whether I'm worth a damn. So here are your choices:

A)   You look in the box and find me dead.
B)   You look in the box and find me alive.
C)   You tell me you love me.
D)   You don't look in the box at all.

A   Don't you feel bad now? I could have made you happy if you let me. But no. I'm dead, and you have your baby, which you'll probably tell a year after it's born that you don't love it anymore, but you still want to be a mother. Let me ask you something. That baby you have in your breadbox—what freakish state is it in when nobody's observing it?

B   Lucky you! Lucky me? We'll have the baby, which I've always wanted, by the way, but you wouldn't know that. And then what? I may be some jobless pothead, but at least I know what makes a mother and a father, a husband and a wife. We ain't it, but you got it all figured out in that smart little corporate brain hiding in your skullbox. You forgot one thing; you don't exist until you begin to examine the choices you've made: the pantsuits, the BMW, the *Wall Street Journal* subscription. All of that a far cry from the pot--smoking, dirty-mouthed girl I met in college.

C   If you could just tell me you loved me, just lean your mouth close to the box, place your fingertips on the surface, whisper into this stuffy darkness—and mean it—there might be some real hope for us. That heart, that heart hiding deep in your chestbox—I believed you had one without seeing it. I thought it was real because you acted like you really loved me.

That's the problem with love: you can't ever prove its existence because the heart's hidden.

D   Of course, you could also walk away and leave me here, go out and enjoy a fake martini with your friends while making fun of me. I'm hoping you won't do that because when Schrödinger dies (it's any moment now), you're all I got, and if you shut me out, I'm nobody. Just a guy trapped in a box.

Are you still out there?

HOMO ERECTUS

Henry's wrist bones shivered with the collision of aluminum bat to skull, a vibration that traveled his elbows, armpits, ribcage, and belly. He looked around the lightless alley behind the bar before bringing the bat down on the head once more. He was about to run, then he crouched beside the body and emptied the man's pockets of the wad of tips. As he was bent, Henry felt stiffness between his legs. He stood and looked down, and there below his belly, tugging at his nylon warmups, was a massive erection.

A noise from the backdoor of the bar sent him running. Before getting onto the street, he removed the ski mask and gloves, desperately caught his breath, then took out his cellphone and pretended he was talking as he walked to his car. The dashboard clock blinked 8 p.m. As Henry sped the backstreets, he squeezed his hand down his pants to investigate. *What the hell?* He punched his leg, bit his tongue, even pinched his scrotum, but the erection was undeterred.

When he got to the YMCA at 8:07, he swung by the dumpsters and discarded the evidence, including the cash. He walked bent over into the Y to conceal the protrusion from the old ladies working the desk, grunting and gripping his back as explanation for his posture.

"Gonna sit in the sauna," he told them.

Once out of sight, he hurried down the stairs to the basketball courts, where five guys were warming up.

"There he is."

"Hey, Henry, whaddaya say?"

"Sorry, guys. I was upstairs getting some crunches in. Been here about half an hour."

"Crunches?" The guys leaned on each other, laughing.

"Can we get this game on already?" Kenny snapped, unamused.

"I'll be right there. I got to use the bathroom first."

Henry rushed through the locker room and into the bathroom stall. He pulled his warmups down, and it was still there, throbbing. *Shit!* He listened for anyone nearby, then proceeded to masturbate. It was inexorable in his fist, and after a few minutes, he quit. He pulled his pants back up and left the stall to view himself in the mirror. The boxers he wore provided no support beneath the thin nylon, and the erection pointed like a divining rod. Henry kicked the door of the stall, then stood listening to the squeak of sneakers out on the gym floor.

He suddenly scrambled to the lockers and began rifling through people's stuff until he found a roll of athletic tape. He pushed his pants down and wrapped the tape around his wide hips, fastening his erection to his abdomen, until the roll was empty. He laughed looking at the mummified penis, then pulled his pants up and checked himself in the mirror. It was unnoticeable. He quizzed his flexibility by raising his knees, squatting, jogging in place, but most of these movements bit into his skin. Henry exhaled and shuffled out onto the court.

"Let's get this over with," Kenny said. "I want to get to the bar before going home."

"Is Kissy working tonight, Henry?" asked Sanchez whose name was Paul.

"Yeah, shit, I'll go, too if Kissy's working," said Walker.

The ball was passed to Henry to inbound. He squeezed it. "Uh, I think she's working. I mean... I don't know." He passed the ball, then hobbled down the court.

"You *think*? Shit, I'd never let a girl like that out of my sights."

The erection swelled beneath the tape. It felt like a whole loaf of deli meat was strapped between his legs. Walker passed him the ball, but Henry immediately threw it off as Big Dave began to guard him closely. A basket was scored, and everyone ran back to the other end of the court.

"Why you running funny?" Albert asked.

"Your herpes acting up?" cracked Sanchez whose name was Paul. "Too many crunches, I guess."

On the other end, Big Dave posted Henry up, thrusting his butt into

Henry for position. Henry quickly backed off. Big Dave was given the ball, and he scored.

"What the hell kind of D was that?" Kenny yelled. "Sorry."

On the next defensive play, Henry couldn't help but steal a lazy pass at mid-court, and he found himself in a fast break situation. Henry was forced to sprint as he and Kenny charged toward the basket with only one defender to beat. Kenny fed Henry the ball near the goal, and he jumped to score a layup. He came back down the court, his teammates high-fiving him, until Big Dave screeched.

"What the fuck is that?"

Henry's erection had broken free, and it was pointing at the guys. He covered it and shied from the court, but not before everyone saw. They moaned and scattered. Walker was doubled over and laughing hysterically.

"Why you packing heat, Henry?"

"It's the crunches…" Henry tried. "I mean, the medication I'm taking, it has all these side effects."

"Get the hell out of here with that shit," Kenny screamed, the maddest of them all.

Henry fled the gym and stomped up the stairs, barking and smacking at his erection along the way. He Cro-Magnoned his way out of the Y, hunching and grunting again for the old ladies. Once in his car, he took out his cell, scrolled through the names, began to call, put the phone away, took the phone out again, and called. He got voicemail.

"Kissy, hey, it's like 8:35. I've been at the Y playing basketball for the past hour or so. I just wanted to call and maybe…come over, if that's cool. So it's 8:35 now—no, 36, and I'll be over in, like, two minutes. I'm just going to come right over without stopping, so…yeah."

Henry dropped the cell on the passenger seat, exhaled, then turned the ignition. He sped back through town, bypassing the street that went by the bar. He turned into the apartment complex, went to her building, walked the hall that always smelled of fried bologna and cigarettes, and stopped at her door. He put his erection under the waistband of his boxers to tame it, then knocked.

Kissy opened the door, eyes smeared with mascara. She seemed not to recognize him, then collapsed on him and wept into his shirt. "What's wrong?" he mumbled, clutching her small body, his erection trouncing her ribcage. She suddenly jumped back, looking at his pants.

"Jesus Christ, Henry."

He began to apologize, until he examined her. She was dressed for work, which meant a black miniskirt that barely covered her panties, a low tanktop and push-up bra, big hoop earrings, lipgloss shimmering on her pouty, Latin lips. The tingle shot through him.

"Henry, why are you looking at me like that?"

He shut the door and approached her. She kept her eyes fastened on him as she retreated.

"I just got a call from the bar," she said, knocking into the coffee table. "Someone killed Rob."

The erection was leaping forcefully as if trying to free itself from his body. Henry pulled his pants down to his ankles and shuffled forward. She ran into the wall, her eyes wide and chest heaving.

"Henry, I think you should know something," she stammered, reaching under her skirt to roll her panties down her legs. "About me and him."

"There's something you should know, too," Henry said, lifting her off the ground. She wrapped her short legs around his waist as he pinned her to the wall. His hands under her ass, he held her just above his leaping erection.

"About what?" Kissy breathed into his ear.

"About me and him," Henry said, and the plunge came next.

ROYALTY

Just out of high school and looking for her lot, Queenie Ladd pursued Big Paul King, manager of the Bojangles' in town. She married him despite his blazing eczema and constant smell of fried chicken and Bo-Tato Rounds. She stayed with him despite his pill-popping and fooling around with Inez, the lady who made the biscuits. And now, four years and twice as many biscuit employees later, Queenie's still with him because, as she'd been reminding her mama ever since she'd quit sleeping on King's couch, "I just know some good luck's coming my way for bringing our names together."

MEASURE OF A MAN

Luke sat at the foothills facing the Smokies for perspective, to be dwarfed, when his flatbed truck couldn't manage it. Nothing could. Quit this gazing. The other drivers might see, might call out his nicknames: Hey, Jolly Green Giant! What's doing, Tank? Paul Bunyan, where's your ox? The belts tightly securing steel rods, and all else looked fine, so he climbed into the rig and jumped out onto the road he'd stare down for the next eight hours. Mostly it was a comfort, the rig for its solace, his talent at moving the massive vehicle about the world with an ease he'd never accomplished with his own bulky hull, some inches short of seven feet and a few pounds shy of 400. Even so, it could be hell when he was nagged by a thought and had 500 miles to chew on it. This time, it was a date with Jessie.

When he got to the station earlier, Randy and his shit-eating grin intercepted him and said, "The new girl wants to see you." He shouldn't have, but Luke went into her office, and she leaned over her desk to make her cleavage known, a tiger or flower low on her breast.

She said, "We should do supper tomorrow. Chinese, maybe? Remember, I do your schedule, so don't tell me you got work."

She smiled in a way to make Luke have to "Yes ma'am" her, and now he tugged his beard and cussed. It wasn't her—she was a fine-looking woman and nice enough. It was about what it was always about, what sooner or later always turned his experiences with women into carnival freakshows.

Jessie was worked up after Luke left a beastly scent and the ghost of his Man behind in her office, so much she had to close her door, shimmy down her jeans, and get herself off. When finished, she fixed her clothes, reopened the door, and sat back at the computer to make busy, telling herself, *Stupid Jessie, that was stupid.* Office clerk at the trucking station was her first stable job in a long time and the best thing to happen since getting sober. For nearly a year, she'd been without alcohol and was still learning what stable meant from her meetings, her sponsor, and, of course, Jesus Christ. In the negative, the definition was easy: not drinking a pint of vodka for breakfast, not getting into fights in grocery store parking lots, not screwing married men and having two boys by the same one, and, of course, not being so drunk that those boys are nearly killed. A framed photo of them sat vigil on her desk, a reminder of what she almost lost and her reason for remaining sober.

Part of her recovery, unfortunately, was also abstaining from men, at least until everything else is in order, says her sponsor. But she's been good. Things are in good order. And Luke's different from the others, a good man, according to his friend; he wasn't trouble, as far as she could tell. She put it together, and it made good sense—she's been good, and Luke's a good man, and she deserves it. The mere presence of him rattled the savage in her and didn't factor into her equation.

After only one hour of staring down the purple mountain road, and Luke had come up with five possible excuses to get out of the date, all of them ersatz to the real reason, which flickered against the windshield of Luke's mind. These were women's faces when they saw it: wide-eyed like child post-nightmare, blushing and turning away in allegiance to Christ, laughing outright, skepticism, probing pubis for prosthesis, then his face for explanation. Only a truckstop prostitute with a vocabulary for these situations gave it to him straight: "Sorry, big boy, but that would put me out of work for a year." Shortly after, Luke had given up on sex and women; it was easier to avoid one by the other. So it was with Jessie.

Then Randy crackled over the CB, "Boy, you better not be setting there, scheming out of that date."

"What you know about it?"

"Did she lean over the desk and squeeze her titties together?" "Aw, shit. I knew you had a hand in this."

Randy laughed himself into a coughing fit. When he recovered, he said, "Come on, man. It's just supper. Just go on and have a good time."

A loud, sporty hatchback came up fast on the truck, accelerated, then nearly cut Luke off. It zipped away into the night, the taillights mocking.

The next night, Luke and Jessie sat at a booth in the Peking Palace off the highway. Dinner buffet-style, Jessie found pleasure in watching Luke empty plates. By the third, she was up at the tins of steaming food building him another meal. There was nothing to do while he ate but keep up or talk, so she talked, and soon she was saying everything she intended on keeping but for the space to fill and his gentle eyes. Then she reached the part of her story she had vowed never to tell again, where her baby boys were up to their chests in bathwater, Mama passed out on the floor. She wept into her palm, repeating, "They saved themselves."

Luke put his fork down, pulled a handkerchief from his overalls, and said, "Sons have tenderness for their mamas, always. They'll have you back when you're ready." Jessie looked at Luke from the wadded kerchief.

Luke liked this woman, maybe even loved her. He loved her maybe because she recalled in him his obese sister from Nashville battling her own addiction: painkillers for her back, or it was his mama who fought to keep a family together, husband and son both in prison for growing acres of cannabis. These women warriors, their tragic stories, fight in them still, so with Jessie across the table moving her mouth around her troubles, Luke's heart instinctively swelled.

Her small hand on his body now had a new reaction, and he took notice of her green eyes outlined in mascara, part-smeared but sexy for it. She had sun freckles on her braless chest, and maybe he spied the dark outline of nipples through white cotton, definitely their shape at least. An awakening began in his pantleg.

Stroking his large hand, Jessie didn't want to wait until the next date or the one after that for sex. She hadn't had a man in a year, and being in the presence of one such as Luke was like sitting before a sweating bottle of Grey Goose.

She tricked him into her trailer with an old standby: there was an ex just out of jail calling, threatening to come by. Would you mind keeping me company a bit? Once in, his size worked in her favor as he was too tall to stand straight. He was still finding comfort on the couch when she was at him, tonguing his meaty mouth and moaning into the hollow, fingering his beard and using it to pull herself to her knees for a better angle. She straddled his leg, her thigh and calf sleuthing what was pulsing. No, that can't be right. She sat on it and recognized it immediately, the heat spreading through her a confirmation. There, between denim and lace, commenced a grinding battle until Jessie's torso entire spasmed and she used God as a verb. Legs numb and fists full of his gruff, she smiled up at Luke. His cheeks were flushed, and his face contorted looking down.

"Let's go to the bedroom," she said. "Let's stay right here doing this."

"Shit." She stood, yanked him off the couch, and pulled him along.

The old anxiety jittered through Luke as he stepped through the small kitchen, the floor whining beneath his boots. In the bedroom, the darkness buzzed, the carpet, wood paneling, and unmade bed each had a smell, the visible slow to follow. This was a familiar room, but so far, the woman was not.

She was thirsty, her stomach doing a dance at the juxtaposition between herself and this giant, every possible move right there to be done, but her chest clamored danger. How would this be possible? Her thigh had memory, and it was now calling out the measurement stained on the skin, big enough to get the attention of her whole stiffening body. The disease reacted differently: the taut chord from heart to pussy plucked, both a tickle and an ache. She pulled her dress off and pushed down her panties, careful to keep watch of him. She was ready for anything now.

Naked, she made more sense as her skin narrated her story, inked with names and skull themes, the type you've learned to quit regretting, scars here and there that you'll always regret. Muscle and a fierce skeleton belied femininity, but her breasts and pubis offered tenderness. Still, she stood before him as though to attack, that hurricane tension before a bar fight. He unlatched his overalls to fall at his ankles and pulled at the button snaps of his shirt to signal that he was ready, though he wasn't. No man ever is; he just does.

The dogs her daddy used to train for fighting in the backyard were taught not only to be fearless before danger but for the danger itself to trigger attack. The bigger the thing set before it, the wilder the dog got. Her daddy got good at building props of bears and lions, and he'd let Jessie help glue on the fur from her stuffed animals she enjoyed skinning. At eight years old, she even helped train the dogs, especially when he was too drunk. It was every day after school for years before she realized she'd been trained, too—fights with bigger, older girls, fights with boys, and now the site of Luke's heavy, hanging enormity set her off.

She came at him; he flinched and might have swatted from reflex if she wasn't so quick. She worked on him wildly, then shoved him down on the bed, and the bed's legs gave, the thump hardly heard for the humming thrill. She climbed him and buried her tongue in his beard, her sour dick mouth. *God, this will happen*, his head sang. With mighty momentum, she rolled off, pulled him, and they were switched, bodies fuck-ready.

Then she spoke words more phantom than form so at first they frightened him. "Be good to me." A sudden suck and white blaze. Stars, actual stars.

She was caught calling the double-o of good, mantra to a meditation that might have lasted hours. There was no feeling, then all feeling, filled up everywhere, until space was discovered.

"Give me some more," she said to his eyes, the twinkle of all she could see. He did. She outright hollered.

"You okay?"

He made to retreat, but she snatched him, firing, "Don't you dare." She took hold of the meat of his hips, and her throat cleared to make way for these words. "Now give it to me, goddammit."

He was being mindful about what and how he gave. He was being good, but her teeth clipping his chest between pornstyle calls—some words, most not—and tugging his beard and hair, his brain switched off for the call of this fuck. His animal was taking over, and it was ravenous.

The pounding rhythm was delivering her elsewhere. She was learning something Eastern, thrust to opposite ends where those ends met. At each stab was rapture, where agony found orgasm, both distinctly felt. Her body told it better: biceps taut, pulling him down, feet flat on his quads in leg-press push. Luke was no more, lost to primal instincts. His buttocks had a surge working, a fantastic urgent pressure, and his body worked furiously to deliver it. She screamed out *Good* or *God* as her whole body said to kick, moving the beast back. The motion resulted in him kneeling idol-style before her, panting. The room's spinning slowed to a stop, and his faculties found him. He found her body like a casualty, legs splayed, unmoving but, thank the Lord, she was heaving. He was completely Luke again; she, too, was another now: a mother with estranged boys, disease for drink, hopes for better than this.

What things he'd done. How he'd treated her body.

"Fuck you if you're pitying me." She pulled Winstons and matches from the nightstand drawer, eyeballs hard on him.

"Sorry."

Lighting and drawing. "Be sorry for that look on your face," each word a chapter of smoke, "not for fucking me."

Now kneeling in the center of this collapsed bed—being in this room, this trailer—grew intolerable. He looked for his clothes.

"Come lay with me."

She shimmied to the side, patting the space newly made. He fumbled to fill it, trying for invisibility along the way. In the crater made by his bulk, their skin touching was unavoidable. He made still.

An assurance itched her tongue, but she didn't have mothering in her, not at that moment, not for the man who just rocked her understanding of sex. *Man up*, she wanted to snap, but smoked hard instead.

No, she'll let him mope some. She'll smoke another stale cigarette, her second in a year. Then she'll summon the man back, a host of ways to do it still to be done.

Riding the shoulder and striking a match for a cigarette, Jessie was on her way to Target for the fifth time that week. The bedroom armchair displayed new blouses, skirts, dresses, and pants, tags still attached, receipts somewhere. Maybe the clothes couldn't make her a good mama to her boys; maybe there was no perfect dress to apologize for her neglect. She was to meet them tomorrow for lunch. After six years, she out-of-the-blue called and too easily convinced their father's grandparents to allow it. It was too soon. What outfit? What to say?

You could say she found herself there, but alcoholics, especially sober ones, are always aware of their proximity to drink. It involved agency to drive past Target, park, deftly purchase, and move the car to a desolate corner of the lot, bottle between her legs like erection. She blasted the radio, but there was no decibel high enough to block the screaming objections.

She was in twisting motion when Luke opened the door.

She was supposed to be at the station like always when Luke returned from his route. The boss was chewing Luke out over Jessie's absence until Luke, panicked, told him to fuck himself and raced off to find her. Not at home and not in the bar nearby, the liquor store in the Target shopping center was the next stop.

She looked at him like a child, but her hands on the bottle were a savage clutch. He leaned over her to turn the radio down, then said, "Maybe I should hold that."

"I think you'll have to take it."

He did in a hard, swift yank. Detached from the bottle, her strength left, and she crumpled into tears. Luke helped her out of the car and into his truck, then drove her home. He made dinner: chicken-fried steaks, corn on the cob, mashed potatoes, and sawmill gravy. He was a wonder with a knife, a wizard with oils, a witch with spices.

"You big son of a bitch," she laughed from the table, watching him work. "I didn't know you cooked."

Dredging steaks, he shrugged.

She got behind him, hugged his belly, and watched as he laid battered meat into the snapping oil. "I'm going to get you a nice frilly apron."

"I look good in pink."

They laughed a lot during the meal at no real joke. They fed each other; she'd sit on his lap and eat off his plate. They were getting up often, getting more, just moving around. She came to the table with two drinks, making no notice of it while telling a funny story that demanded attention. He must have left the bottle in the truck. When did she get it? Still laughing, still playing—he felt too good to care. She seemed okay. She must have exaggerated her disease to be able to drink so casually, make it look so ordinary. Alcoholics don't sip; they chug. They drink in alleys, not out in the open. She wasn't hiding it, so it must be okay. Two more drinks won't hurt anyone. They were hysterical, and his stomach ached from it. He never drank, and he'd never had a better time. By the third round, drunk already, he was the one pouring the vodka.

The playing suddenly turned lascivious. He had grabbed her arm for no reason, and that was all it took. The familiar seduction on her face now spoke meanness. She might have told him to fuck off, swinging her arm from his hold just before grabbing his dick through his jeans. "I want to mash that monster cock," said her mouth, but her eyes didn't say the same. She pulled her shirt off and stumbled to the bedroom. Luke stumbled after.

Staring each other down, sizing the other up, they talked all manner of nasty while undressing; these were nightmarish scenes they forged not even in whisper. The graphic rhetoric riled the leviathans in them, and like things unspeakable spoken, the not-dared was done—smack, punch, choke, and gag, but rapacity remained unfed, so she got on her face, hands pulling herself apart while he stood behind her double-fisting his hulk—where it couldn't be undone ever.

Police siren, fire drill, alarm clock—telephone. You answer telephones. He made his arm reach to the nightstand, pick it up. It was 11 a.m. Jessie wasn't in bed. She couldn't be. She was on the phone.

"I'm in the hospital. Don't come see me."

Phone still ringing. Breathing. Very blue sky through curtain crack. "Did you hear me?"

"I don't know what's going on." "Big fucking bastard."

His brain wasn't working, but at least now it knew to search the room for clues. He might have spotted something.

"I was supposed to have lunch with my boys today." At boys, her voice crashed, but she had more. "After six fucking years, I get to see my babies, and now I can't. I can't, goddammit."

After an interminable whine where he hadn't even context to console, the phone hung up.

It was a stain on the sheets, a bad dark color. A pattern of it went out the door. His truck was not in the drive. Something was coming to him. His heart jerked, and he flung the sheet from his body. That was where the night was hidden. He gripped his fat head and growled to abate the grisly images, but they came faster and didn't quit until he crumbled the nightstand with his heel. The phone lay easily defeated, the dial tone its taps.

Now he wanted to talk to her, ask her how bad, plead forgiveness, but he went back through what she said and found that she didn't want to hear him or see him, and who could blame her.

A sudden fantasy emerged so vivid he dared try it: if he tore the curse clean off, many problems would be solved. There was even a Bible verse for it. He made to do it, but a cautious tug was all he managed. He wasn't man enough, is what it came down to. But what does it mean? After all this time, stacking up pounds and inches, what's the measure of it? Does it measure up? All men knew but him.

There was something she said he could do, but if he thought on it too much, he couldn't do it. He jumped off the bed, staggered into the ransacked kitchen, to the calendar pinned next to the phone. Jessie's scribble said there was time.

He showered, changed, and chugged out into the cool, bright afternoon, the sun hard on his hangover, but welcome. He had another vehicle in the garage, and thank God it had some gas in it. He got in and sped down the highway in the shadow of the mountains where he'll always be small, and the road that runs along them should always be the right road. That's the only wisdom Luke's ever known, and it's still hard to live his life by.

Without hesitation, he charged into the restaurant, bypassing the hostess to scan the booths. There, near the window, two boys sat building a pyramid of coffee creams.

He went straight for them, their eyes widening as he neared, eyes as fierce as their mama's, which said they'd spend most their lives in fights. Runty now, they'll grow to scrappy men, the types who tease far bigger men for the thrill. They'd get away with it, too, since bigger men don't know what to do with smaller, reckless ones. But if they were engaged, unless lucky, they'd find themselves badly broken and meaner.

"I'm Luke, your mama's man."

Jessie was tired of meanness, sick of broken. This was the worst she'd ever known. The gauze stuffed up in her and twenty stitches was the least of it. This might have been the last chance to ever see her boys, her position at the station was probably replaced, she was off the fucking wagon, and her life was ruined again. And Luke—if only she could settle all the blame on him. How easy it would be to blame it all on a man, on a dick, or a bottle. Lying on her stomach in the hospital bed, staring at daytime talk shows where lives should be worse than hers but aren't, she heard herself say, "I should fuck him in the ass." It was in the room, the air, and it came back to her as if said twice, clearer this time and piercing the swamp in her head. The thought grew, took on detail. She was in a porn shop, picking out the biggest strap-on she could find; she was holding it up for Luke to see, fear in his eyes; he was on all fours, and she was giving it to him as good as any man, and he was taking it.

IT MADE HIM STRONGER

Pastor scribbled his sermon in the attic, the screech of his pen cussing the house.

Pastor's wife drifted down the hall open-robed, leaned on the doorframe of Boy's room to find him Bible-reading in his muddy playclothes. Her eyes told him it was time. Boy stood and followed her into the bathroom, waited naked and elbow-gripping as she sat on the edge of the tub and ran water. He knew when to retrieve the minty herb oil and how much to drizzle in; he got the candles from the third drawer, placed them on the vanity perfectly spaced. He left the matchbox out for Mama to make this right with dreamlight. In the spookish giggle of water and steam wisping the dusk like ghostthought, mother and son submerged themselves in the bath, and their skin found its silk. She squeezed the washcloth, heavy with heat, at the nape of his neck; he hummed at it. She scooped out soil from his nails and worked soap into foam to lather his twiggy body, but at the armpits, she tickled him until he squirmed. Sshh. She tipped his head back onto her sternum, poured a drinking glass of water to rinse shampoo away; the suds formed a thrilling line from between her breasts to between her legs. And she prayed. Her forehead on the middle of his back, lips to his birdie ribcage, tears lacing his spine, she begged, *Make my boy strong.* It was a prayer she forced the Lord to keep, spoken every day, twice a day, until one day, after years of persistence, it began. His body swelled between her legs, the wings of his back became half-moons of rock, and his chest grew thready with muscle. But Lord had yet to answer it all. Bashing at the door until it splintered at its hinges, florescence dashing dream, and there Pastor stood before them, crunching knuckles. She was still. Boy scrambled out the tub, bones knocking porcelain and tile, fleeing on all fours creaturely.

She shouted after him, and he halted just at the door. She stood to meet his wide eyes in the defogging mirror, then pushed her breasts into Pastor's dusty sweater and said, "You're not man enough."

She held Boy's mirror-gaze for as long as she could sustain Pastor's fists, and then a blow to the jaw crushed her. In the gloaming of half-consciousness, she glimpsed the furious blur of thrashing arms and heard both grunt and moan but felt no pain. There was peace, and hovering above was the shadow of a man. In the water licking her wounds, the blood was swirling the tub pink like squid's ink. It had been hers, but now, mostly, it was Pastor's, and she soaked in its glorious sermon.

DIAGONAL

Knees buckling and about to snap, torso twisted, wavy-haired head smushed in the corner, Abraham Lincoln's long body is crammed into a too-small coffin. Three mourners stand around the box, gawking at him, but the way I drew them then in the third grade—without knowledge of depth and perspective—the mourners look like they're lying down around him. I meant them to be gawking at the dead president who doesn't fit in his coffin.

The picture-drawing has never been smudged from my memory, and even though I don't have it before me now, I can still see it perfectly: the cloudy, lead-fogged area where my small palm rested on Lincoln's pencil-bearded face as I drew the rest of him, only the idea of the beard and eyes and all that exist underneath the cloud. Recently, the drawing has begged more from me since I rented this costume, slipped into it carefully, treated the cotton blends like ancient skin, wore it around everywhere, and became Abraham Lincoln.

A durable image has stubbornly settled in my brain since that day in school and has existed side-by-side with the coffin. Lincoln is sitting in a theater (there is no drawing of this, not by me), gangly and tall in his reserved box, legs and arms sprawled all over, hanging over everything because he hardly fit in anything. The war is finally over (the South lost), and he's relaxed, despite not fitting. His stovepipe hat is jammed over his knee, Mary Todd's hand nestles in his, and they're watching the play. "Oh, look, dear, I love this part," she says, to which he leans his war-shriveled, wavy-haired head down to his wife, and before he can say, "I'm sorry, dear, but I'm not paying any attention at all," his face is in his lap, or part in his lap, part in his wife's. For a brief moment, before he can register in his mangled brain that a bullet has entered him, Lincoln is sitting upright again, trying to see where the shot came from, looking around without a face, just a Lincoln-shaped bowl of a head filled with bloody stew. Then he slumps over, and John Wilkes Booth leaps onto the stage from the box and laughs and shouts, and the audience thinks it's part of the show—the actor jumping on a stage after assassinating the president. It makes for a strange play, too strange for an audience not to be an audience, and he flees in the night, leaving Old Abe sprawled, then later folded and smushed into a too-small coffin.

And now these images are especially important because, as I said, I was Lincoln (I still am, in a way). They must have been rattled awake on the day I turned eighteen, and then shaken free from the murky bottom of memory when I was dragged back down South from college after not even one semester. I walked into Dr. Kilburn's office complaining of migraines and walked out with cancer after Mrs. Hinshaw threw off her easy way and attacked the doctor who, in her eyes, delivered me my death, took away her only son, and she scratched him good on down his dry, flaky face. Surely these images reflected the fact that things were good for me until that day, that my youngness was just about to transform into a promising manhood. This transition included the acceptance into a bigtime university where I studied philosophy and literature (but not history) and new ideas and knowledge that promised an infinite amount of learning. At that time, I had forever and a fiancée named Jenny who worked on her daddy's farm and drove a sky-blue Ford pickup while her huge mass of frizzy, yellow-white hair poured out the open window. Surely the images recognized this, propelling them to the surface with the intent of providing rations of explanation for me. Once they reached just below the surface, they waited while I found it impossible to live at home with Professor and Mrs. Hinshaw because of the way they and Jenny reacted to my dying. Me, not knowing how to die properly for them, pretended that I wasn't dying, pretended I wasn't aware that everyone else was pretending I wasn't dying—all of which made me leave the Hinshaws and move into my dead Grandma's house down the road. Once there, the images were waiting for me to be alone and wonder what to do with the short time I had left, wondering if I had to act like an old man waiting to die, or if a young baby of a man had to grow a fast beard, white hinting silver, and act wise, pretending that he'd lived a long full life. I was pondering how to be young and old at the same time; the images waited for me to find this fate somehow funny, somehow absurd, definitely unfair that I was being smushed into my coffin far too early (surely I wouldn't fit, they don't make them that young, do they? Even Lincoln at however old he was, didn't fit because he was too long with life). They waited for me, the images—Lincoln's untimely assassination, his murder making everyone think it was a play, his too-small coffin—remained there in my cancerous brain for a purpose, to define the moment when I would become Abraham Lincoln.

After I moved out, I walked down Eli Pass to the costume shop two blocks away on Main Street—almost everything in Victory, North Carolina, was two blocks away from everything else, except for the distant farmland. What we couldn't find in Victory, we could find in Thomasville or Highpoint only ten miles east—and I rented the costume from Mr. Bailey, the only man in Victory who didn't know I was dying because he's a Yankee. No one in Victory talks to Yankees—not openly, anyway, probably because (as Professor Hinshaw taught me) Yankees went sticking their noses in our business, and we Southerners didn't like it, so we seceded, and the Yanks wouldn't let us do that. There was a war, and the Yanks with all their money beat us, and now, here's Mr. Bailey coming down from the North to open up a costume shop in the South, and the town doesn't like it none, Professor Hinshaw said. And who can blame them, Professor Hinshaw asked, though not to me even though I was the only one there. So I rented the Lincoln costume from Mr. Bailey, and he looked at me funny and said he never thought he'd rent this out down here and asked me what I was going to do with it, and I said, "Wear it." He looked at me for a while, then said, "Fifty bucks," and as he handed the costume over to me, he said it was due back at the end of the month.

And then I became Lincoln for a brief time, and then I'll die (but not yet—soon, but not yet).

At dead Grandma Hinshaw's house on Eli Pass, I had privacy, and spent one whole day just being Lincoln, wearing the big long coat and floppy bow-tie, stovepipe hat and glued-on beard, existing as the man in the leadfog of my memory. Sitting at Grandma's small writing desk (Grandpa so dead there was no masculine furniture in the house), stacking old grammar books, falling- apart Bibles, and time-broken dictionaries high around me (simulating a scholarly setting like Professor Hinshaw in this study with his books, and this one big fat book), I balanced my bristly chin on my fist, assumed a Lincoln- esque pose, and tried to imagine how he felt. I pretended those clothes were his clothes, and in the lining of the fabric was his actual skin with his real nerves, which attached to mine, new, red-threaded nerves entwining with old dusty ones. In my desperate hopes, there was one that bubbled up haphazardly from the thick tar (the primordial soup of the brain, from where everything comes—not to be confused with the carcinogenic tar that was born from the tarsoup Lord knows when) and settled itself precariously on the surface; it was a hope—like I said, a desperate, haphazard hope, arising at a frantic moment just before telling Professor Hinshaw and not Mrs. Hinshaw that I was leaving the House, going down the road to Grandma's to die—that simply dressing as Lincoln would solve everything.

By existing in his clothes, in his skin, in his nerves, by sitting before old books in a chin-to-fist pose, by muttering the few words I knew of the Gettysburg Address (*Four score and seven years ago, our fore fathers, in order to form a more perfect Union*—), and then, by writing Lincoln-letters with a shaky hand, by assuming the only identity left for me to connect with, the only identity truly symbolic of my plight, I thought my premature death might magically burst with meaning. I didn't know how the other young and dying did it (are there others besides me?); which roles did they take up—Washington, Santa Claus, Spiderman? And when I was writing the Lincoln-letter to his (my) sister in that shaky penmanship (*Dearest Sister, the War is almost over and I gave an address today at Gettysburg and I'm going to the theatre tomorrow but I think I'd rather chop down some trees...*), I felt the pain—a sharp pain running from the right side of my skull to my shoulder, like a cord of electricity that bolted up and down each time I breathed, which sent a memory quick and steady into me. When it came into being as a memory, I don't recall ever having forgotten it, like it was always there, and I always remembered it being there so maybe the lightning pain was a jolt to surface the memory. But after that moment of pain, my mind could only focus on this memory, which was a new Lincoln image, and I let it play itself out:

Lincoln in the forest, in a smoky forest, barefoot and barearmed, barechinned—no beard—a pool of smokefog sliming his feet and legs as he whacks at oaks with his rugged axe, felling them left and right, and the rhythm he keeps with his whacking is hypnotic and relentless because he never slows, never quickens, only swings with his axe in the forest continuously.

I could practically feel the cold sweat of the fog on my legs as it slithered by me—the memory, the image hauntingly real, cold and wet. I came to a conclusion then, a thought that inspired action in the strange way that the physical obeys the ethereal, that the origin of this vision was a picture, and there seemed to be a kind of commentary made on it—like something read, and not just read to me, but to many, almost condescendingly, or at least to impressionable, undeveloped minds. So finally, as I sat at Grandma Hinshaw's small, feminine writing desk, I realized that the image I had of Lincoln came from a picture book that was read to me and my third grade class (the last grade of public school before my homeschooling began). I realized the other two images I had of Lincoln also came from this book, one that Miss Westmoreland read to my class. At that point, my muscles flexed; they wanted the book. I wanted the book. The old, dusty Lincoln nerves attached to mine wanted the thoughts that would inflate the clothes, the skin, the nerves, and make physical Lincoln-flesh and bones to inflate my bony death with fleshy meaning. I wanted the book because there might be more there, more that I could identify with, or just more details to the former pictures (now a powerful triad of images) that would inspire the kind of wisdom that the older, more silvery, white-bearded men have to accompany their death.

Professor Hinshaw had an entire library of Civil War books (he calls it the War for Southern Independence), all of which were shelved in exquisite Southern Academia fashion in this dark mahogany study at the end of the hall. He spent most of his life in here, the inside of which I've seen only three times (not counting now—sitting in here writing). Once was an accident when I was seven, when I was exposed to a haunted room where ghosts were summoned by an obsession with the past: ancient books layered the walls, save for where tea-tanned maps of battles and a magnificent oil of Jefferson Davis hung in great glory. Two battle-scarred flags—the Confederate's and the Union's (the latter being more damaged)—silent like skeletons of soldiers on each side of the desk. The huge desk was a pool of milky brown wood with an antique lamp that fuzzied the study with soft-orange. Scattered papers were strewn about and this book lay open (I should probably capitalize "book")—this Book lay open, over which Mrs. Hinshaw, disrupting the room's ghosts, was bent. Professor Hinshaw was in midthrust. He shrieked at me—his mustache drenched, his otherwise elegant lion-maned hair darkened by sweat, matted against his shoulders and chest—and Mrs. Hinshaw looked up at me, her thick, brown hair twisted atop her head in a bun, except for one fat curl escaping. Her brown eyes slanted at me in embarrassment, then suddenly became soft and kind as she smiled at me, so as to show I wasn't in as much trouble, as sweaty Professor Hinshaw shrieked. She pushed back into him, I remember. The tiny splash of golden cross bounced back and forth against her large breasts, heavy like water balloons. She trembled and watched me, smiling, understanding something I didn't, but making me feel good and funny, and Professor Hinshaw shrieked a second time for me to close the door. After that, I had to stop calling them Mama and Daddy.

The second time was a year later. This time I purposely entered, and I met a calmer scene: Professor Hinshaw, dry, quietly studying this Book. Looking like a Southern general, genteel yet delicate, his hair was pulled back around his smooth, pretty face, which hosted a perfectly groomed mustache. I showed him my picture-drawing of Abraham Lincoln, diagonal in the coffin, lead-fogged face, and he glanced at it and stared at me for a long, uncomfortable, impossible moment, then nodded at my drawing and said, "That's real nice, boy." Then he told me to leave him alone and called for Mrs. Hinshaw who escorted me out of his study while smiling at the picture of Abe I showed her; I felt funny but good about my drawing's authenticity, since a scholar of history and a scholar's wife approved of it.

The third time was only a couple days ago when I entered deliberately, and Mrs. Hinshaw was there again, but this time, she was sitting, clothed, and clenching a tissue, which she quickly hid. She smiled at me, but not the funny good smile; it was a forced, broken smile, one that revealed the constant anger in her. I firmly told her to leave, and she had to because the men needed to talk. She obediently, yet elegantly accepted her powerless role, and I told her to shut the door on the way out. I told Professor Hinshaw to sit down in his very own study, the one he forbade me to enter my entire life, and I told him plainly that I was leaving to die on my own at Grandma Hinshaw's because that was the only place I could go. He could do nothing to stop me, and it was difficult because he always protected me; he sent me off to college when he felt I needed to escape (but forbid me to study history), he kept Mrs. Hinshaw from me when he felt she wasn't behaving, and I'm sure he kept me from this study because there was something in here he felt would harm me. I wasn't leaving because I was angry, but I was firm, and I had him bent over this desk, and no one was smiling.

If I needed a book on Lincoln then—probably even a children's book—I knew exactly where to go, but I had seceded from the Hinshaws. They would not let this be for long, however; they would again seek me out to restore the Family—and I would seek them out too. I decided I would never return to this study, nor this House, again. It was more than the awkwardness I felt dying in front of Professor, Mrs. Hinshaw, and Jenny that made me leave. It was more than the forced smiles, the fake strength, the pretending, the baths, and still more than the fight and what Jenny became afterward, which I was forced to juxtapose with all she was before, especially the first day in this House, last summer. Her hair was blazing from her head like ropes of white flame where she stood on the front porch in a tank top and cut jeans, the bronzed arms and legs of an athlete, hands deep red from handling cattle and greasy machinery on her daddy's farm. Her face was vibrant and pure with beauty, eyes anxious and determined, when she stood there on the porch before me and Professor and Mrs. Hinshaw, then she stepped through the threshold of our House. At that moment, she was the bravest creature in Victory because Jenny knew what she was getting into. Jenny handled herself well with Professor and treated him like a man; she treated Mrs. Hinshaw as well as she could, often like the woman whom she'd be replacing. Something intense but hidden had occurred between the two of them. We escaped to my bedroom where I was exposed to a second naked female form to rival the first, yet Jenny looked the same clothed as she did naked; there was no real mystery in what her body would be like. I knew her breasts would be that muscular, her hipbones that jagged, even her pubic hair that wild well before she shirked her clothes. She moved in on me quick and rough, perhaps expecting me to resist; she bit and scratched me and handled me like a calf, and then, just as I thought I was going to lose my virginity, the fluffy snakes of her hair slithered down my chest and tickled my hips. She peered up at me from below, her eyes green and feral. Jenny gave me the first of what would be many blowjobs.

It was late November, and it was still hot and bright and the sky Tarheel-blue (and it's not that color in New York City, only in North Carolina). I walked through town to get to Levi Ridge Elementary. Victory already heard of my dying because the Hinshaws were absent from Victory First Baptist, and when anyone in Victory doesn't attend church (except for Mr. Bailey who is a Catholic) it gets noticed, especially the Hinshaws. In their absence, the collection basket looks empty, and the women don't have Mrs. Hinshaw's un-Christian dresses to quietly scoff at ("This isn't no fashion show, look at how low—" "Sshh, she'll hear you!"), and the men don't have Professor Hinshaw's genteel beauty and prissy ways to condemn under their breaths; no one has the husband and wife's queer relationship toward each other, the way they walk and sometimes talk like each other, to silently rebuke, and after the service, the entire Church has no line to form before the Hinshaw's pew so Victory can greet them, smile big at them, sometimes ask them for money, always so polite.

So Reverend Perviance, using his weekly Sunday night phone call, which was usually used to thank Professor for his generosity with the collection, investigated the situation. When he visited us the next day with Mr. and Mrs. Overcash and Mr. Tyndall, carrying a basket of fruit and potted flowers, looking devastated, and singing Holy Ghost songs right then and there on the front porch, Mrs. Hinshaw answered the door. I could see the fierce thing beneath her easiness rattle with fury as she glared at them all like she had known all along what they were saying about her and her family and that, this time, this act of kindness wouldn't be tolerated because everything was different. She said to them, "Ain't no holy ghost going to save none of us now," and her choice of "us" confused me because it not only included me dying, but it seemed to put Victory in a similar category. I wondered if it included the Hinshaws as well—"none of us"—, and Mrs. Hinshaw slammed the door on them and forced an unstable smile for me who was standing there next to her. She ran down the end of the hall, fighting to keep her composure, closed the study door quietly, and used her creeping-up fury on Professor Hinshaw. They hadn't heard of me like this, though, the dead boy dressed like Lincoln leaning into town, black hat and coat against Tarheel-blue, which must have mucked up their system of always knowing before seeing. It was a system of preparedness that gave Victory its order, its Christian Order, its Old Southern Order. They never expected a Lincoln in that Order.

The McGruider Brothers were the first to notice me as they were the first to notice everything that came through Victory. They were the watchmen, the guards of the Order. They sat in front of their auto shop all afternoon and evening, big, slow, quiet men sitting with intense purpose below a neon sign reading *Only Jesus Saves*. They watched me carefully, glaring from the shadows of their meshed hats, hating me calmly, like I was pulling some prank on the town, on the Brothers who cherished their heritage seriously—probably more so than anyone else (except for Professor Hinshaw, but that's different). They immediately hated me, calmly, with somber, relaxed shoulders, unable to do anything but hate, a hate that would have sent me running if I was still afraid of the living and breathing. Everyone else reacted more obviously than the McGruider Brothers. The town did share the Brothers' sentiments, as trucks and old cars had bumper stickers that said Heritage Not Hate, or If At First You Don't Secede, Try Try Again, or even just the old Stars and Bars. As I walked on down Main Street, the few people in cars stopped right there in the road to stare at me, and Reverend Perviance who was talking to Mr. Tyndall outside Walker's Pharmacy stopped in mid-sentence, his mouth agape, watching me walk by as if I was a ghost. As I strolled past Lola Mae's Salon, I saw Mrs. Overcash try to stand while under the chrome curling helmet to get a better view of me through the window, and all of the old men having their afternoon coffee at Strobel's set their cups down quick and eyed me suspiciously, something dusty in them getting worked up. They pulled their pants up over their bulging bellies and walked outside, and Mr. Bailey even stepped out from his shop to see what was going on, but he only found me funny and went back inside. I think everyone gathered and followed me, but it was hard to tell since I focused solely on getting to the school.

I am tall, not as tall as Lincoln, but over six feet, and I must have appeared even more absurd in Levi Ridge Elementary this miniature world made for miniature people, ducking through the doorway, my stovepipe hat skimming the ceiling. The kids who passed in their perfect girl-boy lines giggled and stared (I stared back because their life was just as absurd), and the teachers looked just as shocked as those outside, but they were more reserved about it, trying to keep the children quiet.

I wandered around the cramped halls, not sure if I wanted to go to the library or if I wanted to try to find Miss Westmoreland's classroom. She herself wouldn't be there because she was fired right after I was removed from Levi Ridge and I was made to sit at home while Professor Hinshaw taught me math, science, and philosophy—no history—and Mrs. Hinshaw taught me French and literature—women's subjects, she said with a smile—and I hardly ever left this House. It didn't take me long to not want to leave, but to want to continue these lessons, for I had a hunger for knowledge, a curiosity to know, just as I wanted so badly to go into Professor Hinshaw's study and read all of these books in here. But Professor was hardly here anymore himself, not since he nodded at my picture-drawing and pulled me out of school, and he strictly forbade me to come in here. I knew that I couldn't disobey him because of the deathly serious way in which he demanded my obedience on the issue.

And then I saw him there in the hallway, just as I thought I might, the little boy with messy hair, but he didn't recognize me, didn't even seem to see me because he was walking quickly. I followed as he bounced on past the multi- purpose room and the gym; he seemed preoccupied with his little hands, balling them up in tight fists, then opening them and wriggling the fingers before his face. He barged into the bathroom and came out two minutes later, slapping a paper towel about those hands in guilt, like he did something bad, and then I remembered what he was doing with his hands, with his cleanliness. Mrs. Hinshaw had a fascination with both, a caring attention to my hands and to cleaning me and giving me baths everyday. She began doing this again a few weeks ago because I guess she was angry at me for dying and she couldn't understand how her son could betray her so completely, divorce himself so absolutely from her. So all she could do is bathe me, like she used to sometimes more than once a day, all the way up until Professor Hinshaw wouldn't let her anymore, when he sent me away to college. She returned to it, drawing my bath and tying her thick brown hair off her bare white shoulders, stained with blood-splotched freckles, and taking her time with my cleanliness, smiling easy, the way she used to when I was in third grade and thereafter. She'd take my hands into hers at the end of the day and whisper, "I want you to tell me everything your hands have done today." The easy smile combined with the splash of golden cross on the white, freckled skin of her chest made me want to—have to—tell her everything, slowly as she commanded. We both acted as though I was in trouble and she was scolding me, and yet she kissed my hands, and when I finished telling her, she drew me a bath and cleaned me. This continued until I was in my late teens when Professor Hinshaw intervened and informed both of us in his pretty voice that I'd be going far away for college,—he said it like he had rehearsed it, made up his mind long ago—and Mrs. Hinshaw only listened to him because he was a man, only in comparison to her, and she had been born in the South. Now that I was dying, she must have felt the rules were different (they were), and she once again began to bathe me. I let it happen because it had always happened, since the beginning of time, since forever. I was part of the bond that made me a Hinshaw, part of the secrets that made our family strong and different. So at that time, when the baths began again, when actions became furtive again, I went along with it, not to preserve the secrecy, but to preserve tradition, for Mrs. Hinshaw's sake. I felt guilty for dying on her, breaking the trust, injuring her faith in love and God and family, and if all that could be preserved by a harmless bath, then Amen.

Jenny didn't like this at all. Jenny was not slow and easy like Mrs. Hinshaw; she was quick and tenacious and had always been in competition with her. Jenny hadn't the luxury to be reserved like Mrs. Hinshaw. She was a ripe sixteen and had calculated in her relentless mind that she wanted me, she wanted a Hinshaw, and she felt she could have me, as I was quiet and impressionable and, at the time, afraid of leaving the South and entering the big city for college. She moved on me on Easter Sunday and she had to be fierce because to date me would be to enter the Hinshaw House and Jenny was only one girl, a girl with her daddy's truck and a plan, and she had to be fierce to survive the Hinshaws. Lord knows she was brave to enter by herself and Lord knows there would be a time when she wouldn't walk out of this House, not on her own. But Jenny did love me, despite her calculating plan to get me to propose to her; she loved me more than she ought. It seemed she didn't love me but loved something far deeper than me, like the idea of me, the origin of me, and all I was left to do was let myself be loved in that way, for I could not reciprocate since I didn't know her own beginning, her own essence.

I didn't even know her sex because she kept it from me, kept her virginity, but did not keep her lust. Jenny kept her perfect Southern belle flower, but did not keep her dignity, and she would use her mouth on me and expected nothing in return. She would use her mouth and I could only let her do this for it was beyond my understanding why she would act so slutty ("Do it to my face") yet feign the desire to preserve her body in some Southern tradition. While these strange acts of physical love occurred, I could feel Mrs. Hinshaw hovering about—not spying, not even physically present—but feeling her ghost in Jenny, like she was somehow Jenny's beginning, Jenny's essence, and Jenny must've felt this too, felt that I felt this, because she tensed whenever Mrs. Hinshaw was physically about. The two females were like animals instinctually knowing the other to be the enemy, stepping stealthily around each other like lionesses, with me in the middle. When Jenny found me in the bath with Mrs. Hinshaw, the careful watching turned into bitter growls, and Jenny must have gained some courage while I was away at college for she called Mrs. Hinshaw a name that hurt even me. Mrs. Hinshaw's latent wildness, the essence I could always sense—the scent of a sweating beast— which always laid just beneath her easy and slow façade, kicked in, and she pounced on Jenny taking half the bathwater with her. Mrs. Hinshaw grabbed Jenny's big, frizzy hair and yanked her down on the bathroom floor; she smacked and scratched her good across the face and would have clawed and maybe bit her to death if Professor Hinshaw hadn't held his wife back. Mrs. Hinshaw calmed herself, dried off with a towel, took cotton balls and perox- ide from the cabinet, and carefully nursed Jenny's wounds. I helped Jenny out of the House, and the next day I spoke to Professor Hinshaw (telling Mrs. Hinshaw to leave us alone), and told him I was leaving.

In the empty hallways at Levi Ridge, the messy-haired boy with his per- fectly expensive cardigan and slacks looked in my direction. His mama's dark brown eyes saw Lord knows what—perhaps the Lincoln he'd become— but whatever it was it frightened him and he ran off down the hall, shoes *clap- clapping* on the linoleum floor. He turned the corner in the direction of the library, but instead of going in, he scurried farther down the hall into a wing of classrooms where I caught the tail end of his cardigan disappear through a door. I followed him into that classroom and stepped through the doorway just in time to see him sitting down at his desk in a room full of students; Miss Westmoreland was reading to the class. She hurried toward me, and I thought she was going to say something to me—which I deemed somehow possible—but instead she reached for the door handle, and I moved inside the room as she stuck her head into the hallway, looked around, then quietly closed the door. She began reading again; she sat up on her stool right before the messy-haired boy who sat in the front row with an open notebook, a pencil in hand, and his little, chubby face resting on his little, dirty hands. He seemed to be barely paying attention to Miss Westmoreland who appeared to be reading directly to him, holding up the book to show the pictures to the class, but giving him the best view. There was teenage Lincoln in the forest with his axe (the sound of him whacking on the trees); the boy glanced up at this, and Miss Westmoreland continued reading in muffled sounds— the whole scene was muffled and muted, diluted by a sheet of fog—about Lin- coln's presidency, the Civil War, freeing the slaves, the end of the war, and

Lincoln in the theater (the boy tapped the pencil on the page, not looking up). She read about John Wilkes Booth (the boy, how could it be so vivid to him when he's not even—), the assassination, Booth leaping onto the stage, and Lincoln being carried out of the theater, and his body being brought into a boarding house where they found a room and laid him on the bed. I got a sick, sick feeling just then as I watched myself put lead to paper and pull lines across the page as Miss Westmoreland talked about mourners looking into the coffin, a sick sick feeling as the boy got enthusiastic about his picture-drawing. Miss Westmoreland closed the book, smiled wearily at the boy, and I fell backward against the door, wanting out. The entire room, save for the boy, looked sharply at me; I scrambled for the handle, pulled it open, and raced out of there heaving and frantic. I stood in the hallway for a wild moment, then made for the library in a dash.

The young children who were sitting Indian-style on the carpet before the librarian, Mrs. Lowell, burst out into laughter as I came rushing inside. Mrs. Lowell looked up at me in a kind of horror, the kind that accompanies the sudden perversion of logic, and she stood up to me as the kids laughed and my eyes raced around the little brightly colored room full of books.

She asked me, "What are you doing here?" and I went to find the book. She followed me and asked, "Are you a reader for the children?" even though it would make no sense in Victory to have someone read Lincoln unless that person wanted to get fired (like Miss Westmoreland). I scanned the shelves for History or Biography, and the children laughed. I found the book, and Mrs. Lowell finally recognized me and gasped; I gravitated toward the children as I flipped through the pages of the book almost wildly, hand trembling, book itself shaking so that when I reached the part—the part about his assassination, after his assassination, the carrying him out of the theater and into the room and lying him down on the bed—the words bounced on the page so that I could hardly read them, but I did. I read out loud, and Mrs. Lowell sat back down. The kids listened as I read fast, and then I skipped over it and had to read it again, then again. It was just a phrase that I needed, just a phrase that I read two thousand times over in that library until I could believe it, and then I only almost believed it as the book fell from my hands. I got cold and sick and I groped for the door to leave as Mrs. Lowell said still in shock, "Kenneth Hinshaw? That really you?"

At that point, I was terribly afraid. I knew where I needed to go, and I knew that waiting for me there, besides the ghosts, besides the deep mahogany air, besides the three distinct memories (three fossils of me imprinted forever in that wood), was the source of this entire, horrible mess. I was afraid, yet I yearned to get there—here—to where I did not belong, where I was never allowed. It finally made sense why this room was forbidden to me, because all of the secretes lived here, the phantoms of people long-past fluttering about the darkness like moths around Professor Hinshaw's bent head, around this Book that always occupied him, the source from where the ghosts came and to where they sought to return. Return to the Book. I wanted this Book.

As I walked down Main Street, it seemed like every resident of Victory was not only following me, but pushing me on: Reverend Perviance, Mr. and Mrs. Overcash, Mr. Tyndall, (was Miss Westmoreland really there?), even the McGruider Brothers— following me past Victory First Baptist, Silers View Road where few people other than Hinshaws have ever been—stomping on the gravel road (like the sound of a whacking axe). When I got to the House and raced up the steps to the wrap-around porch, all of Victory stopped, and they waited silently, intimidated by this House—a mansion to them— twenty-foot bleached white pillars could easily look like fangs to them, and the huge doors behind those fangs, a sweaty black mouth. Victory stood in the shadow of the Hinshaw House, as they've done their entire lives, and they shuddered at its mere presence. I knew they would not go in with me, that I'd be doing this alone, though I had no intention of doing it with or for anyone else anyhow, but they remained in that windy shadow (the wind picking up, getting excited with all of us), and they nodded me forward. I walked inside.

I knew there would be nobody home. I just seemed to know it, like it was a morsel of knowledge born in me from the beginning that would reveal itself when the time was right, when I was ready for it. Now I'm sensing that it's all this way, that my entire life, past, present, and future is contained inside my weakening chest, in me from the beginning, and only Death has made me sensitive to it, ready to become aware that I needed to be in this study; I was drawn to this study, as I was my entire life. I'm thinking (writing) now that it wasn't curiosity. I'm thinking now it was something much greater, something I belonged to, something withheld or simply lied about as Professor Hinshaw lied about my picture-drawing, nodded at it artificially (forcing me into this identity), verified the drawing's authenticity right here in this room—a room where truths were falsified and protected, so, logically, a room where they must also exist.

I pushed open the weary door as the wind screamed from outside, and the blackest brown engulfed me. I stood in it, at the mercy of the emptiness—the lack of forms—and was forced to insert the images using my memory. At first, Professor and Mrs. Hinshaw were sweating over the huge desk—Mrs. Hinshaw smiling easy at me. Next, I was handing Professor my picture-drawing of Lincoln, which he studied in silence, then smiled and nodded at me and pushed me out. Finally, I had my bags packed and told him I was leaving to die—and then my eyes adjusted and the books shined through the darkness, the maps, the Davis painting, the tired flags, the enormous pool of rich wood, a single lamp, and the Book. The Book was so still, yet seemed so powerful, larger and more obvious than the memories I had of it: a huge hunk of rust- colored pages, a thick skin of leather, and the faded gold seal raised up from the cover, cold to the touch, an H in a circle. I moved around the desk, sat down in Professor Hinshaw's leather chair, saw the study from his eyes, and felt hypnotized. I could have stayed in this chair my entire life if I gave in to the trance because it was such a powerful feeling to be in this position, but I needed to break open the Book. I stuck my thumb into the dirty meat of its pages, right inside toward the end, and I opened the Book as it moaned and creaked in anger. Before me was a long, ink-blotted scroll laid out across the two pages in perfect lines (nothing like the falling-off lines I'm writing), filling the entire page, more ink than golden brown page. At first, the lines, the penmanship, seemed indiscernible until I read the very first word, and as if reading that word were some magical password, that I had broken some code, everything on the page became block letters, and I could read it all easily, because, as I now know, this Book was waiting for me to read it. The first passage detailed a story I couldn't understand. This author seemed to know the story all too well, and most everything was implied. There were names that kept creeping up—Eli, Levi, Elias, and the most frequent name, Siler—all of a town called Siler Cross, and this passage spoke of a seemingly awful burning and a shame this author bore heavily. His language and lamentable tone indicated he was somehow responsible for the burning, but no other explanation came. I reached the end of the page, where the hand was shakiest, and it was signed Everett Hinshaw, some month, 1967. I turned to an earlier page in the Book, and met with a similar hand— long and shaky— and read the same names, Levi, Eli, Elias, whom, it was mentioned, fought in the Civil War, in the 42nd North Carolina, Davidson County Company, and only one son returned, but it didn't say who. This author was trying to explain some kind of miscommunication, a letter the surviving son sent his daddy warning him about some General Sherman— this author spoke of the letter and, as before, the handwriting became precarious by the end, by the time he wrote *The Union never came*, and signed it Sylvester Hinshaw, 1933.

Further backward I flipped, knowing I should have begun in the beginning, as stories need to begin, but also understanding that there was something big here, bigger than me, and that I had to ease into it. I had to be careful with this truth lest it overtake me (the wind cackling, the whacking rhythm), and I turned over Sylvester's signature until I reached the next name, Jasper Hinshaw, 1910. I read that passage, having an idea of what information needed to be satisfied—a burning, a miscommunication—and this one, this Jasper had the heavy tone like Everett, a burden and a shame, yet in that tone was also determination. In this tone, he spoke of his great-grandaddy—no name, just Greatgrandpa Hinshaw—who went crazy with sorrow at the loss of his two sons, Levi and Eli, and Jasper went on and on about this sorrow, the complexity of such a loss and the loss of his beloved South and his town and his hard work. He spoke of how such a loss could create such a sorrow, such a heated, adamant sorrow, the kind that could justify anything, and Jasper ended on that. I anxiously skipped the rest of Jasper's lifetime of entries because I was realizing that each author, each Hinshaw, seemed to be focusing on one distinct element of this single event, like it was assigned to them somehow, so I understood that if I kept reading Jasper, I'd keep reading about sorrow.

Further back, now nearly an inch from the beginning, where the pages were brittle as November leaves and smelled of rotting memories, I turned the pages carefully, yet anxiously. There was a miscommunication, a burning, and a sorrow that justified something; I came to Ephraim Hinshaw, 1885, who had a thick, heavy penmanship, the words more inkblots than cursive (but it was all shockingly clear). I imagined him an obese man with a thick beard and a lead hand, and I read from him cautiously, knowing he wrote his words with dense meaning—each one a brick—and I could be bludgeoned if I read too fast. Ephraim was assigned the burden of detailing the Catastrophe at Siler Cross, as he called it, where the entire town was burnt down; the crops, houses, and church burned (slowly, I had to read with caution) all in one night. These homes were torched, Ephraim, the large burly man with wet eyes wrote, heaving, lips pressed tightly to hold it in—I could see it all in the ink. The entire town was torched, and Siler Hinshaw himself did it, ordered it, ordered his slaves to do it, the entire town—at night, Ephraim again stressed—and when his slaves had finished, sparing only one House, Siler Hinshaw ordered his slaves, his property, inside the old barn with their torches still aflame. He locked them in there, and here Ephraim gave in, the huge heavy man exploded with grief and it showed in a great big black splotch of ink, whereafter, after he composed himself again, he wrote, *This is what I have to vindicate.*

I was beginning to understand what was going on, yet I also understood how deep this went, and Ephraim was telling me I had to keep this deep inside me, where it was born. I had to hold this silent and deep like a swallowed brick, keep it sacred, or just keep it, and with that I turned to the final lump of entries, which was the first, written by Elias Hinshaw. His hand was sturdy and elegant and I could not guess at its emotion, for he wrote plainly in an indifferent tone, and in this tone he gave the simple facts. He told of father, Siler Hinshaw, tobacco and cotton farmer, owner of many slaves and of many miles of land he called Siler Cross, a place where he let people settle for a yearly fee. A rich, proud man, he sent his only three sons to go off and war with the Yanks to protect his land and his town, his slaves, his South, hearing only one year later that his eldest son, Levi, was killed in Richmond, Virginia, and his next son, Eli, died of typhoid in Wilmington, North Carolina, only three months before the war was to end. At this point, Elias sent his daddy a letter, a short three sentence letter (it was attached), telling his father that Union General Tecumseh Sherman was on a violent march up from Atlanta, Georgia, which he burned down, to Columbia, South Carolina, which he also burned down. Sherman destroyed towns and crops and cattle, freeing the already emancipated slaves that the South refused to give up, and he had recently entered North Carolina where he might march straight through, perhaps through Siler Cross, but the 42nd anticipated meeting him in Goldsboro. The letter was a warning of what might be, only a possibility. Elias tried to make clear in the entry, getting defensive, at which point Siler, already grieving to the point of madness over his sons' deaths and even angrier about the losing situation of the Confederacy, and still ever proud, burned the town himself, not wanting any rich, nigger-loving Yanks to have the pleasure of doing it. The Union never came.

After this, Siler draped the Confederate flag over his head and shoulders, tied the Union flag around his neck, and hanged himself from the balcony of this House, his body still rotting from the noose three months later when Elias finally returned from the tragic surrender and found Siler Cross in ruin, his daddy dead, and his mama and sisters only God knows where. After this account, Elias said that he was rebuilding Siler Cross, renaming it Victory, and that he was slowly accumulating folks desperate enough to take up residence on the tragic land, and he himself was searching for a wife *strong and self-willed enough to bear the Hinshaw name.* He ended with an order: each Hinshaw is to have only one son, and each Hinshaw man is to bear the name's history with shame, but also with the hope that the events of the past can be vindicated, that the name can once again be as noble and proud as the greatest names of the South, and that no Hinshaw will rest until the name is made pure again. He signed his name boldly, like a true Southern gentleman, Elias J. Hinshaw, 1865.

It was windy that day when Siler received his son's letter and he torched his own town, his own people—I know this, I can't not know it as the wind shrieks like a banshee through the 150-year-old House, because I was somehow there, and I am somehow responsible, like all us Hinshaws. There was one more author I hadn't yet read, the one I skipped, the one I read right before beginning my own version: Professor Hinshaw's. I turned to the last entry in the Book dated 1992 and signed Jackson Hinshaw. It said *It ends here, with me,* followed by something like, *Kenneth is not fit, he's not right, he's different and he knows it and all of Victory knows it and he would abuse this knowledge, this name, so it ends with me, and when he's of age, I will send him out of the South, and at least the name, however still defamed, will keep some dignity*...It must have been windy that day.

He sent me out indeed on that Easter Sunday. Professor stood up there in church after the service, held me by the elbow, and told all of Victory in his pretty voice that he was sending me off to New York University. Everyone looked confused—or was it anger? It was that very Easter Sunday that Jenny first came up to me right after church, when she must have sensed my own confusion (or was it anger?). Jenny looked at me the way Mrs. Hinshaw did, but she acted on that look; the rest of the hot, dizzy summer was a sexual rassling match, but with her mouth imitating her other hot hole. She gave me her face, but never her body—she put me in embarrassing, bestial positions, but kept my virgin innocence intact. For all the friction between her and Mrs. Hinshaw, I now see the troubling relationship: Mrs. Hinshaw must have scared Jenny good into keeping me unsexed, and Jenny obeyed faithfully. Why? Perhaps the reason lies with my first experience in this study, when Professor and Mrs. Hinshaw were still Daddy and Mama, when Daddy had Mama bent over this desk, and her hair was tied up tight on her head, like she was… a boy. Yes, because Professor cannot be the kind of man to enjoy the act of sex with a woman, and Mrs. Hinshaw can't be the kind of lady to submit herself to the grotesque act with that kind of man. And that must be where I came in—the man of the House, or at that time, the potential man, one that could be shaped and molded into the perfect man—if I was wet enough, soaking in a bathtub for eleven years. Yes, she must have seen the man I would become, at seven, more masculine than her own husband, and she wanted my sexual energy—wanted it soaked in bathwater, liquid flowing from between my legs to between hers, a sexual understanding that only a mother can share with her son. It's not incest but love that began in her womb and should be taught by that same body, and if it was dirty, the bath would cleanse our souls of the sin. Then there was Professor catching us in the tub, hitting her across the face (she must have liked his aggression) and telling her—not me, though I was there—that he was sending me off to New York (she must *not* have liked that), and the very next day, Easter Sunday, he told Victory the very same thing, almost in the very same tone. And yes, yes they were angry. He knew Victory had some hope in me to treat the history of this town differently, and he wouldn't have it. Victory must have had hope in me from the beginning, yet I'm not sure why (the fact that I have Lincoln all over me shows their instincts were right). It makes sense, though, that they were angry, and it makes sense that they are outside this House at this moment, waiting on me to finish. Of course it does. Here's six generations of Hinshaws trying to justify an event that should just be apologized for. But because of these endless years and lines of inky theories, Victory's trapped in this history of Hinshaw language. Of course they were angry, though they applauded. And now they're waiting for me to stop writing and put an end to all this mess.

    —Kenneth Hinshaw

I leave the Book open to let the ink dry and push away from the desk when I feel a tickle on my earlobe. I wheel around to see the stained rebel flag keeping still, pretending that it hadn't just reached out and touched me, next to it the faded Union flag, both stained with Siler's damned soul. I scramble away from them, from the study, the House.

Back outside among the wind and the distinct, weary faces of Victory, looking up to me for the next move. I know what I have to do, and I walk through them, splitting them open down the middle, heading towards Grandma Hinshaw's. The three need to see me, and Professor especially needs to see me with Victory at my wake, and Victory needs to show themselves to the Hinshaws (all the ghosts will be there) to tell them *No more, no damn more.* We walk in silence, our stampede of footsteps absorbed by the hollow earth road. The house of Grandma Hinshaw is in view, and the specks of Jenny, Professor, and Mrs. Hinshaw run out into the yard. This will make an impact on us all—this strange scene. They will remember it for a long long time, long after I am gone. It needs to be this strange to replace the tragedy Siler Hinshaw committed. Now these people, this town has their scene; they even have a brand-new story in writing. In the Book, I've written myself into words that can be read by desperate people and arranged any old way to say what they need to hear. Like Lincoln diagonal in his coffin, entirely wrong, entirely false.

But it's too late now, too late to return to the House and tear up the pages. And so what am I left to do, standing before Jenny, Mama, and Daddy, their faces scrunched up in pain? Victory behind me, waiting for their fate to change? I can only think to warn them, leave them with something honest before I'm gone, and I'm leaving quickly. My knees give, and I find myself on the ground, the three standing over me and looking down. I can barely see them through the blurry cloud, the fog looking eerily like smudged lead. Their voices are drowned out by a deafening rhythm—an axe whacking away at an oak, but the swings are slowing, the oak is winning. I need to find my voice in all this before it's too late, before I'm taken without leaving that something behind. And as I open my mouth, I feel the tightness of the glued-on beard clenching my jaw, but I find the words.

"He was in a bed. He was diagonal in a bed."

WAR CASH

Since returning from Iraq where he sustained shrapnel to the brain, Bridges jumbles his words, making a simple request to the attendant for a car wash an unintended political remark.

DEATH FOR YOUNG LOVE

To do it right, to make pure the omen, we'd share the kill. Our first as a couple to be wed. We wait. We are good at waiting.

From a perch in a tree, it sees their young hearts catch like the embers of a nascent fire. It sees people-heat, not their pink faces or their loose skins the color of forest rot. The deer sees heat.

Quivering near the rifle, we breathe out through the nose, our eyes on the glorious beast, God's great reward for our patience. We are slow and quiet.

It knows, by the speed of young hearts, that its death is coming—it's a violent, sexual pounding, a passion for destruction that glows white-hot as Creation. It steps into a clearing under the pouring midmorning light and tips its head to graze the burdock. It waits.

The shot ignites in us a fire. We fall on each other and thrash. It's happening. We fuck—fuck with the rifle right there between our bodies, fuck without grunt or gasp, without thrust or arch, so that on the altar we can tell God we waited.

The spirit, entangled by its sinews, soul netted in cartilage, feels the fight as exultation, not pain. In the dirt, a chorus of sparks from the tree where the two dig into one another, grinding bone into bone.

In our garage, with the sweet smells of oil and cedar shavings rising from the bench, we work on the carcass, our arms sleek with blood, slimed by organs up to the elbows. We use our grunts for skinning, fuck-noises for butchering; we use our newfound desire on the tonnage of shimmering pink flesh. We look at the head, the impressive antlers branching from the skull. Our knees on its neck, blade to bone, we saw and sweat.

Its flaming energy throbs in the jagged nub of its bone-branches. It's been reduced to this, to be held by young hearts. Now it is a part of their story.

THE MULTITUDE

The young couple walked the neighborhood street, newly plowed after winter's first big snow. The sidewalks and driveways were unshoveled, waiting for people to return home from work to this chore, an hour's worth at least in the night soon to come. A pickup with a rusted plow sped toward them. Douglas maneuvered himself to the outside of his wife. Usually, she was amused by the new protective behaviors he had adopted since she had become pregnant. He half expected her to slide her arm through his and press her coat-fluffy body to him.

They'd just returned from the hospital. The doctor had explained what the bright spots in the ultrasound meant. They were on the baby's heart. The words were hazy in Douglas's head—tumor, cyst, Downs—as though they had sunk into the ghosty part of his thinking. It wasn't that he didn't care, he had explained to his wife; it just took him longer to process. It scared him as much as it did her. His wife began to cry again, and he searched his pockets and found an old fast food napkin. He handed it to her, but she ignored him and walked a few steps ahead. The snow began to tint pink, which said the sun was gone and evening would come, and the next time he saw a car it might have its lights on. Two driveways ahead, down the crest of the street, an old man was shoveling. He wore an ear-flapped hat and a red flannel coat. He worked the shovel deliberately—a shallow scoop and walk to the edge and twist of the blade. Only a small segment of asphalt peeked. The old man held the shovel limply as they passed. Douglas felt sorry for the man and made the mistake of looking into his soft, blue eyes. "Want some help?"

After Douglas said this, there was a quiet moment when the world didn't respond, and he was relieved that he might not have said it. The moment gone, the old man said matter-of-factly, "Yes."

For the first time, his wife stopped and faced him. She searched his eyes as if for recognition, not rage but outright wonder. He looked at the old man to free him, but the old man was waiting, leaning on his shovel.

"Jesus Christ," she muttered and walked off.

"I'll...I won't be long," he called and then stopped. The sound of his voice was pathetic. She was moving away quickly, and at one point, she slipped, and her arms came out of her pockets. She found her footing and continued on, more determined to get away.

"'Nother shovel's in the garage."

Douglas expected the old man to be grateful, but he continued shoveling. Douglas sighed and turned toward the garage, high-stepping the snow to get there. He got the shovel, and when he turned back to the driveway, he was alarmed to discover how noticeably darker it had become, rendering the old man's form pixilated and dreamlike. He rewalked his steps, snow leaking into his boots and biting his ankles, his cheeks hot with cold.

"I'll take this side?"

The old man said nothing, and Douglas sighed and dug into the job. Douglas worked as fast and hard as he could, not even looking where he was flinging snow. Soon, the hems of his jeans were globed with ice. It was getting darker, colder. The snow on lawns was now purple. This the loneliest time of day.

Where was she now? How long had it been? He had no watch, and his cell was in the car. Their progress on the driveway, a quarter of it cleared, didn't translate into time. He shoveled faster, feeling the ache in his hamstrings and back.

A commotion from behind made Douglas flinch, like someone was running up on him. He turned around and saw mysterious movement across the street. A multitude of dark forms were taking shape against the shadows. Their lithe, liquid movements mimicked the noisy silence of nightmare, causing Douglas to step back even though he was far removed. They broke the shadow of the house and came in full to the yard, a herd of ten or fifteen deer. The old man coughed and, at once, all heads and ears perked, and the deep, black eyes steadied on them for a long moment. Douglas held his breath, fearing that even a careless thought would trigger something unimaginable and terrifying. Then, in unison, they continued their creaturely trek, stepping the snow in a casual line toward the street. At the curb, the large, antlered leaders dipped their thick necks as if quizzing the space, then eased out to cross the street into the yard that belonged to the old man. So easy and fluid were the deer's movements that Douglas's heartbeat found its native rhythm. A double-flash at the summit of the street froze the stream of crossing deer. A car's headlights illuminated the snow's spin and glowed the deer's black eyes white, and the car, too fast for this neighborhood and not slowing but horn blaring, crashed into a pair of the animals, hurling one as if shot from a cannon, gripping the other into the grill. The car screeched and slid a few yards before stopping. The other deer hightailed off into the shadows. Douglas heard only his own whimpered breathing. The mangled heap of creature meshed into the car's hood was motionless. The part of Douglas that knew death knew it was dead. Cutting the cold, aluminum air was the stink of exhaust and musk. There were sounds of life coming from the flung deer. It raised its head and jerked its neck to get its rear off the ground. Its front legs were working, but the back ones were not. It dragged itself for a couple of its own lengths, collapsed, then tried again. The body dragging and thudding and the scrape of hooves on ice echoed through the still neighborhood as if on a soundstage. What scared Douglas most was that its eyes reflected no anguish—that if it were chewing grass or nosing its doe, it would look the same as it did now.

"Check on the driver," whispered the old man.

Douglas forgot about the driver. The air bag clouded the view through the windshield, though on the steering wheel he might have seen a hand, a knuckle. He got no farther than the old man's mailbox, still a good ten yards from the car, when the dead deer suddenly collapsed from the car's grille in a sickening thwump. Douglas's stomach leaped, and he fell backwards into the snow bank. There was a rattle from the deer's hoof that clattered the street. Spooked, Douglas scrambled to his feet and sprinted madly away, the old man yelling after him.

He wasn't sure where in the neighborhood he was, other than back the way he had come with his wife. His boots too heavy to carry him faster and the ice slicking his steps, he must have looked crazy-legged drunk to someone watching from a house—though at this time of the evening, there would be no one home.

ON THE PILLS
(RIDING THE LONG, COOL WAVE THROUGH THE DARK GAP)

7.5 mg/325 mg oxycodone and acetaminophen (Percocet); 5 mg/5000 mg hydrocodone bitartrate and acetaminophen (Vicodin); 5 mg hydromorphone (Dilaudid oral liquid); 60 mg oxycodone (OxyContin); 50 mg meperidine (Demerol); 65 mg propoxyphene (Darvon); 30 mg codeine sulfate (Codeine); 60 mg morphine sulfate extended release capsules (Avinza); fentanyl citrate lollipops (Actiq), and 50 mcg/h fentanyl transdermal patches (Duragesic); 5 mg methadone hydrochloride tablets (Methadone); and, preferably, 40 mg Methadone wafers.

Off the Pills (Paralyzed by Paradox in a Broke-Down House)

I am stuck in the Dark Gap, unable to move an inch. Movement, after all, is a paradox: for anyone to get from point A (the bed) to point B (the kitchen, where the linoleum floors are warped and the sink drips and drips), one must first go half the distance from the bed to the kitchen (say, to the bathroom, where the tawny ceiling sags from water weight) and, to travel to that halfway point, one must first traverse halfway to that halfway point (the off-balance dresser, to put on shorts and T-shirt) and, before that, halfway to that halfway point (feet on floor, the tickle of air breezing through the splintered hardwood), but first, halfway to that (from my crooked back to my cagey side), et cetera, et cetera. There are an infinite number of halfway points and, therefore, I cannot move.

Substitute the Pills (Renovating Broke-Down House, Filling Gaps)

10.1 oz. acrylic latex caulk plus silicone; ½" x 8'4" moisture-resistant drywall; 10 oz. liquid nails, heavy duty construction adhesive; 12 oz. Big Stuff gaps and cracks foam sealant; 1 qt. spackle paste int/ext; four rolls of self-adhesive, fiberglass drywall tape; 61.7 lb. pail all-purpose joint compound; 6" x 75' butyl rubber with polyolefin film facer flashing tape; 30 year, three-tab charcoal shingles; 150 sq. ft. roll granular surfaced leak barrier; 5 gal. asphalt flashing cement; 10 ft. traditional white vinyl style gutter; 6" x 3' mill hinged gutter guard; 3" x 10' rust-free aluminum round corrugated downspout; 9 oz. white advanced gutter and flashing sealant.

Back on the Pills (Renovations Complete Except for One, Giant Crack that Can't Be Sealed)

10 mg/650 mg oxycodone and acetaminophen (Percocet); 10/660 mg hydrocodone bitartrate and acetaminophen (Vicodin); 8 mg hydromorphone (Dilaudid tablets); 80 mg oxycodone (OxyContin); 100 mg meperidine (Demerol) tablets; 65 mg propoxyphene (Darvon); 60 mg sulfate (Codeine); 90 mg morphine sulfate extended release capsules (Avinza); fentanyl citrate lollipops (Actiq), and 75 mcg/h fentanyl transdermal patches (Duragesic); 10 mg methadone hydrochloride tablets (Methadone); and, always, forever, 80 mg Methadone wafers until the walls fall away.

TELLING THE SAMPO

2 October, 1982

Dear Liz,

I am here, and it's just as I remember it: birch trees everywhere, same smoky smell to the autumn air, and the people still shy as teens. Forty years later, and nothing's changed except me.

Matti's brother Paavo picked me up from the airport. I wish I knew ahead that they looked exactly alike—I thought Matt came from the grave to spook me back on the plane, back home. Seems like something he'd do. But their resemblance is only physical. Paavo might as well be mute, even by Finnish standards. His wife, impossibly, is even quieter. The silence is welcome though. I'm not here to talk.

Paavo drove me around Keskusta this afternoon, and then we went to Oulu Univeristy where he teaches. For a man who doesn't talk, he somehow opened his big mouth about my coming. When we got to his office, every member of the English dept. was there, fawning in their strange Nordic accents. I had no idea they'd know me way out here. But don't worry, Liz, I was polite. I smiled and signed their books (which, apparently, were translated into Finnish. That's news to me. I'll have to buy a couple before I leave.). I was not okay, however, when they began inviting themselves out to Paavo's cabin, the place where I'll be working. At this point, Paavo stole me away and marched us down the hall, apologizing the entire drive back as if his tongue were stuck in a loop. Jesus, I miss you. Writing you from this distance, from any, is horrible. I haven't written you a letter since, what? High school? It feels that way; missing you this much and writing about it feels adolescent. A cold stone in the stomach.

Listen, I know my coming out here raises all those bad memories. You didn't say anything—always the goddamn gracious wife, you bit your tongue, helped me pack, kissed me good-bye. I feel like a bastard, so you know, for leaving the first time and leaving now. What can I say except Matt's death awoke some things I need to sort out. I know that sounds stupidly mysterious, but it's a mystery to me, too. When I figure it out, I'll explain it all.

This is when I say I love you. Regrettably, this is when I apologize.

Tom

16 October, 1982

Dear Liz,

Thank you for the package. The circus peanuts were a hoot. The only candy they eat here is actually salty—they call it salmiaki. They do, however, make a good liquor flavored the same way. Paavo and I have become good friends over it.

Your timing is perfect, as always. The package came in time for me to wear the knee brace on our hike near the Russian border. I tolerated the walk well for an old fart, but I'm sore in every crick today. Paavo tried to get me into the sauna (every house here has one) to help the pain. He doesn't understand why I won't go in, and I don't know how to explain it to him.

The other day, I picked up a book called the *Kalevala*. It's Finland's version of the *Odyssey*, a very strange epic poem that oddly enough speaks to me. And to you. Here's a passage from its beginning:

> Long my tale's been in the cold
> for ages has lain hidden:
> shall I take the tales out of the cold
> scoop the songs out of the frost

bring my little box indoors
the casket to the seat end
under the famous roof beam
    under the fair roof
shall I open the word-chest
and unlock the top of the ball
untie the knot of the coil?

Your last letter made it clear that I should not take the tale out of the cold, or at least that I should keep my trap shut about it. Perhaps you're right. My attempt at honesty is selfish. But the poem addresses another. You asked who came out here, the writer or your husband. You know how to hit it, Liz. It's both. Your Tom is all knotted up in this, and I've come out to untie him.

The first snow of the season has just begun. The flakes are the big, fluffy kind, like cloud chunks, and the sight of them riddling the gray afternoon reminds of the days with you and the kids along Chittenango creek. I think I'll brace my knee, tough out the pain, and take a walk. I will bring you along.

Much love, Tom

31 Oct, 82

Dear Liz,

Not surprisingly, I was atrocious over the phone. It was great to hear your voice but awful to listen to myself bumble assurances. Hell, I'm sorry, Liz.

Let me clarify what I was trying to say on the phone. First, I'm glad you're reading the *Kalevala* as well—it bridges one of many gaps between us. The parallels you drew between me and our epic hero Väinämöinen may be accurate, but be assured: my quest here will not last an epic period of time. I don't intend to start and finish an entire novel while here. I'll be lucky if I even start it! And while I admit to having some demons to exorcise, I will not turn that into a mythic saga. So I'll repeat the date when I'll be coming home: February 15, in time for my birthday.

Tomorrow, we set out for the excursion I came here for. We'll be staying in Paavo's family's cabin near the Norway border for the remaining three months. And, yes, all the Finns from the English dept. are coming along. I decided they may be of some use after all. Unfortunately, the cabin is too remote to receive mail, let alone electricity or running water, but Paavo assures me there's a town about ten miles away with a post office, so when I get there, I'll send you another letter with the new PO box address.

Liz, I hate myself for putting you through this, just as I hate the sound of my apologies, like Paavo stuck in a loop. When I return, let's go somewhere tropical, perhaps Hawaii or St. Martin. We'll sit on the beach and drink cold beers under palm trees and talk of nothing but nonsense. Conjure this up the next time my stupidity fouls your mood. Lie down to bed with it at night, and so will I.

I love you, Tom

1 November

Liz,

Eleven of us van-prowling through Arctic twilight, steady line of purple snow racing out the window, distant mountains gradually growing. Meanwhile Abba and Meatloaf blare from the radio, Finns singing along happy or oblivious.

I am here.

Have you gotten to the part in the *Kalevala* where Aino drowns herself because she was forced to marry Väinämöinen? Her mother was so leveled with grief, her tears forming rivers, sprouting birches, birches keeping cuckoos who call out reminders of Aino's fate. (And our hero Väinämöinen, broken by grief.) I wake up to cuckoos, Liz.

Survival here is a basic struggle. We hack away at wood, we haul lake water from a hole axed in ice, we shovel walking paths, we shiver in bunks, then add another log. Then there's downtime: a scary Nordic beast—3 hours of daylight, noon to 3. Candles always going oranging the commons room. The Finns, they play cards, they drink hard, they use the sauna, and they are fascinated by me. I don't know what they will do when those things wear thin. Me, I am thrilled by the conditions. There's time to write and read. Time to experience and fiddle with knots. To study cuckoo song. Then there's time to think late at night when the Finns sleep and cold creeps and my mind wanders into the woods, passing through trees, trudging through snow, peering down the slope at the frozen lake listening for the stirring beneath the ice. Listening too hard.

The candle wax is a puddle, the flame going. This is not the way I wanted to end the letter. I'll give you a better one next time.

Yours

11/82

Dear Liz,

Thank you for the photograph—that catfish is nearly as big as Ryan. I often wonder what creatures roam this lake. Nights, I stand on the ice and peer into the hole expecting to see the spiny back of some prehistoric lake monster. The water is blacker than anything you've ever seen. It stirs up the imagination, and it scares hell out of me. There's folklore to water, a timelessness that intrigues (ever wonder why we've always lived near it? either the ocean or the creek?). This lake is thick with meaning—its story sung in gurgles, poetry its only interpreter. Väinämöinen couldn't translate the song and suffered the grief. Then he had his second chance in his arms when Aino took mermaid form—he was about to carve her up for meal, but she rebuked him for not recognizing her and swam off, this time for good. My second chance may be slithering out of my arms as well, standing too much on the ice, peering too long into the hole.

I did not write you drunk, Liz. You caught me in the early stages of adjusting to the Arctic element, so I'm sorry for the bad poetry. Cabin living is especially challenging. We wake up after sleeping in sweaters and pants, cut wood to rewarm the cabin, fetch water, make breakfast (which consists of very strong coffee and makkara, or sausage, maybe a slice of dark bread and a hunk of cheese if any's left over from the once-a-week trip to town), downtime, maybe a hike if it isn't snowing, prepare sauna (it takes a couple hours to warm), eat dinner (sauages, bread), sauna (not me, Liz), downtime, bed. Even for the Finns, this cabin is too unrelenting. After only two weeks, two of the ten have left, perhaps because my novelty wore off. Ironically, it's Petri and Sirpa, the two American Lit. professors—they exhausted their questions about my novels. I honestly don't know what keeps the others, for what keeps me is entirely different. Unless we all have our lake monsters.

Love, Tom

P.S. You still reading *Kalevala*? What the hell is this *Sampo* Väinämöinen seeks?

12/82

Liz,

No, I don't have the Oxford edition, and I'm glad for it—the translator's conclusion that we must accept the Sampo as mystery would cause me to chunk the book into the fire. That's lazy interpretation.

It's been vibrating my brain alert at night; I've been going over and over its few appearances in the epic: In "Forging the Sampo," dejected Väinämöinen meets Louhi, mistress of the Northland, who promises to return Väinämöinen to his home (and his sauna) as well as bestow her daughter on him, if he can forge this Sampo. He tells her he hasn't the ability to forge it, but he knows the smith who can, Ilmarinen, the one who crafted the sky. Väinämöinen brought this challenge to Ilmarinen who took it up, persuaded by the maiden gift, and after four failures—forging a crossbow, a boat, a heifer, and a plough—finally forged the Sampo with its triumvirate mills: one for corn, another for salt, the third for money. Once finished, Ilmarinen faced his promised maid, but she turned him down, saying she had work to do in her own land.

Much later in the epic (in "Stealing the Sampo"), Väinämöinen, Ilmarinen, and Lemminkäinen steal the Sampo from Louhi when Väinämöinen lulls her army by playing his kantele. They take it on their boat, and Louhi sends the fog, which Väinämöinen disperses with his sword. Then she sends the sea-monster, the Gaffer's son. Väinämöinen threatens it, telling the monster never to return, to which it agrees if spared. The poem then shifts to fable, saying the monster has never since, and never will, show itself to mankind. This is the strange story of the Sampo.

My poor companions are being bombarded with *Kalevala* questions. If they gave me better answers, I'd leave them alone. Only Paavo and Anja are Scandinavian Lit. professors, and both teach the theories of the Sampo you mentioned but don't have a particular opinion (or don't care to tell me). Pia, the only historian, will talk extensively on the subject (usually after the vodka's open), but it always shifts into shouting about Finland's independence.

One request does get satisfied nights, however, and that is to have the *Kalevala* read to me in Finnish. This is typically done by either Paavo—who seems to feel some guilt at not having more to offer on the subject of the Sampo—or Tipu, the one grad student who came along for some sort of credit and, as such, is willing to do just about anything no one else wants to do (which includes reading to me).

It's a spell, Liz, a haunting chant. I sit back in the firelight and listen to the crooked cadence, the cumbersome, mesmerizing music, imagining meaning into the words, each pronounced syllable triggering an action in the epic, tickling the prehistoric part of my brain that understands this language. By the conclusion of the reading, I feel wiser on the subject, but hardly smarter. It has become my quest to demystify the damned Sampo once and for all. The other night, I finally braved the first step.

I've been avoiding sauna this entire time. (Perhaps you've noticed?) Well, I took it on, much to my group's delight—they've been pressing me about it nightly, and my acquiescence might have actually delayed many of their leaving. It was a difficult return. You know how it feels, Liz, to visit a childhood place after decades of absence (neglect) and how the smells— perhaps the pine of a grandmother's yard, or the must of the back of her closet—rip you back so hard and fast your stomach rollercoaster aches? It was the very same, triggered most mercilessly by smell: the cedary red-olence of hot wood, the burning scent of steam, the violent transition of lake water tortured upon scalding rocks. But there's more to it than smell. The sensation of enduring pain in the form of heat, sucking fire into your lungs, water pouring out your skin as if bleeding it, posturing your body to tolerate the heat, the pain, the sweat. This is an ancient ritual for Finns, and yet it's personal. An internal struggle.

Still, the Sampo remains somewhere at the bottom of that lake. My nights remain busy peering into the hole, cursing my fear. (Is this something I can even tell you about? I question everything I tell, since you scrutinize the slightest slip of my pen. Hopefully you won't begrudge sauna description; I desperately want you to know at least something I'm experiencing here.)

Yours, Tom

Liz,

I couldn't wait for your response to write again. I've been thinking about the idea that sauna is the only way to include you, and since I did not describe it right in my previous letter, I'm going to give it another try.

I'm taking you in with me.

The ritual begins late afternoon. It takes a couple hours to get the rocks good and hot, so you have to start packing the stove with wood to get the fire going early. The ones assigned to this chore will also fill all the pails with lake water for ladling. Then you eat dinner. On occasion, some of the Finns have taken their makkara into sauna, cooking them in foil on the rocks. Then, a snort of cognac or vodka to warm you up, and it's time.

As I've mentioned, sauna is in a separate cabin, just up the slope. As we walk over to it, look down to your left and you'll see, through the trees, an imposing field of ice arresting the firs. You'll also notice, reflecting off the frozen lake, a motion of colors—blue, pink, and green—and perhaps, if we pause our march, you'll hear a cosmic whisper above our head. If you catch a break in the trees, you'll glimpse the Northern Lights swirling the sky. Long ago, on a night like this, Matt told me the legend of the lights: the Great Nordic Fox swipes snow up into the sky with his tail, and what we see are the flakes catching the moonlight. This has always married itself to the image of Matt (and many many years later, his younger brother Paavo), hacking away at the ice with a long axe, the noise of steel to waterbone mixed with a grunt, and leaping up into his face and into the sky, icesplinters by the thousands.

Just inside the cabin, in a small room on the left, is where you remove your clothes. It gets tight in here when everyone's undressing at the same time— knees and elbows knocking. So you feel more comfortable, I'll introduce you to everyone. It's an unnecessary formality, as you'll truly get to know these people when suffering heat as a community. Regardless, this is Paavo, Anja, Saana, Outi, Erkki, Kimmo, Pia, and Tipu.

Before we enter, prepare for how hot it's going to be. If at any time it becomes too much, just step out on the porch and cool off. It's not a sign of weakness. There's no reason to try to prove yourself in front of the Finns. (I know how stubborn you can be.)

Ready?

Feel the wave of heat wash over your face, down your shoulders, your arms, torso, legs. It feels good, like getting into a hot shower after working out in the cold.

Right now, you're probably very aware that you're naked, and you don't know where to settle your eyes because you want to look at everyone else's body—not out of any sexual desire but because it gives you a more complete picture of that person. Nothing is hidden now, and you want to match the color of one's eyes to the shade and size of her nipples, the thickness of one's fingers to the girth of his penis. You want to look but know you shouldn't; neither do you want to appear uncomfortable, making it obvious that you're not looking. All I can tell you is in a few minutes, you'll be distracted by the heat.

The first ladle of water is poured on the rocks, which will fire off a scorching steam. You'll notice how focused you are on the pain, on your breathing. You concentrate on your fingertips, watching sweat bead off, but the heat keeps coming, and then it plays with your mind. You hurt, so all the hurt you've ever experienced is recalled. While you're not alone in sauna, you're alone with pain, and sometimes it beats you and you have to leave; sometimes you win, but it's only a victory for that night. It starts all over your next visit to sauna.

This particular night, I stepped outside for a moment to piss off the porch into the snow. You are there with me, young and exotic. It's December deep in the Arctic Circle, and we're completely naked and standing in the frozen world, sweaty arms locked up, feeling magical with the cosmic light folding above us. We are in love for those moments. They are the quietest moments I've ever known. And then they were ruined.

Liz,

My prematurely-sent letter has thrown off the order of our correspondence. I'm not even sure to which you are responding—I don't think it was the most recent. If I had any sense, I'd wait for you to catch up.

I need to keep writing you.

We're a sweaty herd stamping down the slope toward the frozen lake where the sky's spectacle reflects phantomlike on the powdery surface. We aim for the black blemish, a hole axed in ice. We crowd around it, waiting for the one who's done it before, Paavo (brother of the one who did it first) to show us it can be done. We are filled with crazies, laughing and terrified.

He plunges in, and we crowd the hole to steal a glimpse at the disappearing act, holding breaths. Only a second later he resurfaces, gasping and shrieking and *holyshitting* in his language, leaping out the water, disappearing off the ice, up the steps, back into sauna.

It can be done. Could it be done again?

My turn is coming as the others imitate the first. There is little thought as to how this will work. The madness, the cold coming, the feet sticking to ice, and the lights slithering across the sky make it hard to think. And then I'm alone, the last one, standing with my toes curled over the purple-white lip of hole, staring into the roiling black eye of the lake. This is when my logic returns and reminds me of the danger, tells me to fear. There are things in that lake that have been waiting for me, and there's no telling what they'll do.

I step off the ice and plunge in.

This is where things go black. How do I describe it to you? What lake words but *bubble* and *deep* do I know? This logic gap needs filling, for when I tell you that the Tom who comes out—who limps off the ice and up the slope and who settles back in sauna gasping for air—is never the Tom who went into the lake, can you really believe me? When I say, therefore, your Tom is not returning, can you understand?

Dear Liz,

Thank you for the Christmas gift, but by now you know I can't take the Hawaii trip with you. It troubles me to read your optimistic letter, written before you learned I can't return. It is strange to hold an artifact containing your bliss, while, at this moment, on the other side of the planet, you must be in turmoil.

And yet, what do you know? Nothing, because you won't let me tell it. So I have to find another way.

The lake—I'm being a coward, splashing around on the surface. I need to go *down* if I'm ever to get it right.

Submerging—the muted roar of water rushing ears, the squeeze of volume resisting displacement, slicing assault of cold colder than ice, and then submersion—the strange peace of drifting in this Stygian underworld. This is when my eyes come alive because I'm searching, because when the body disturbs the ancient water, the maze of bubbles blazing with northern lights mesmerizes the magnificent ice ceiling that glows and pulses shades of pink stupefies. But down is where I'm drawn, to where even my wildly treading feet are lost in the black. How many millions of miles deep, how many prehistoric monsters below: stirring lake giants snapped to attention—a translucent eye popping open, a meaty flipper pushing off the muddy floor—slithering up toward the pale, squirmy intruder? The physical dangers don't concern me as much as the phantom leviathans ghosting around in the depths, the cursed souls barking out their rages, blackening the water. This is what I baptize myself in nightly.

What I encounter when I submerge, Liz, is a stupid boy who fears me and fights me and flees deeper into the lake every time I draw near. The shadow of his retreat and the scorned expression when our eyes meet are enough to shy away. But I've never been good at shying, so I return again and again, having to dive deeper and deeper to find the boy and try to yank him out. He's been too long freezing and searching in these waters, afraid of the change that's awaiting him on the surface. The last thing he saw was a braid of golden hair twisting down into the pitch, and he's forever grasping at it in his nightmares.

But this is hardly all of it, for I'm contending with all of my selves who have made their visits previous nights, frozen in the quantum fabric of the lake. I have to wrestle through them each time just to begin searching for the boy. These Toms are thick and tumbly at the surface, daft as manatees, battling themselves for space, crowding the hole in the ice, making it increasingly difficult to get out. But there is always hope. There are always the lights to show the way out, either dazzling the bubbles or pulsing the ice pink.

When I emerge, however, as the first time, and I crawl off the ice and make for sauna, I am never the same. This, I need to make clear to you. This, I have not yet begun to make clear. Another time, another way.

Tom

Dear Liz,

Deeply, painfully sorry.

Maybe I *am* writing in metaphor; it's hard to tell anymore. But, regrettably, my meaning is literal. Of course, I can't call. To do so, I would have to leave this lake, drive into town, and I cannot leave this lake. Faithful Paavo, the only one remaining, goes to town to deliver/pick up mail. The problem lies more in talking than leaving. I'm overwhelmed with all these possible ways to tell you what I need to tell you, all of those ways wrong but all ways that could crowd each other, block out any language, and there I'd be on the phone, mumbling out the dissonance. I'm sorry, but writing you is all I can do now, and now even that is failing me. But I'm not surrendering. I still have the fight in me.

Coming out, I swam for the lights—a ladder of color bending in the black. I would have never gotten out otherwise. Then again, I didn't come out. As punishment, the lake took me hostage, and this other Tom crawled out of the icehole, alone. My gasping echoed on that expanse of ice, got lost in the firs, my fingers changing colors before my eyes. Recalling nascent instincts, I knew to get off my hands and knees and walk. I knew where to walk to: sauna, warmth. The lake was slowly pouring out of my ears and untinting my eyes, revealing a sudden stinging reality. I was moving, alone, transitioning to take up the new Tom who was waiting in sauna for me to slip into: head drooped, shivery, crying into his frozen fists like a baby mourning the loss of the womb.

I waited too long in sauna that night. Truth is, I didn't know how to go along as this new person and held out as long as possible. Then I did leave, went to the cabin where the others were fast asleep, got in bed without saying a word, somehow slept, awoke before the others seeking evidence of dream. I visited the lake, and the hole was frozen over.

I could tell no one, Liz, not even Matt. The story was at the bottom of the lake, wrapped in a braid, my tongue frozen dumb. I left that place, returning—up to recently—only in dream. When I got back, I went back to you, and we married. If it never happened, I would have never come back. I still don't know what to make of that.

Dear,

I should have never taken you down I forced you I lost you losing you. You've become more than girl you've become folklore you've become cuckoo song and mermaid you've become Sampo. But you were once a girl I lost.

Down the slope steps hand in moist hand sky ablaze with foxtail dazzles the young writer finding his experience. As a group, we'd done it the night before. Seemed simple then—in and out like penguins. Now we are alone. Sauna heat is leaving us, cold coming on. Ten toes curled over the lip of the hole. A black mouth stretching its icy jaws to eat up two.

Ready?

You say no. That's what you've been saying, but I haven't been listening. I've been dipping you into the lake night after night, each attempt at telling a tale sunk you deeper. Losing you, and now I'm chasing two braids both retreating quickly into the dark.

Then hope arrived, handed over by faithful Paavo (he's leaving tomorrow with or without me). It was your letter, your words. I've been reading them aloud for the past hour, a saving mantra. These words especially:

> And then there's the other part of me, the one who would spend the rest of her days trudging through the snow and ice until she found her man, wherever he is, whoever he became.

Trudge at me? Trade in your Hawaii ticket and trudge at me, as old as you are, as lost as I am? *No.* I'll find my way out—I'll follow bubbles, paddle toward ladder of light, pull myself up, stand alone on ice, an old man, a son- of-a-bitch writer on a layer of ice no thicker than his phony novels, a son- of-a-bitch husband shaking by his wife's words "trudging" "rest of her days" because she wants this last walk to be with him not at him even if it's walking off this ice together, hand in hand, toward sauna.

I was trying to tell it when it didn't have a language. My whole life it's what I've been trying, but it can't be told. So I'll do what the bard did at the end of the epic after speaking so long:

> I'll wind my tales in a ball
> in a bundle I'll roll them
> put them up in the shed loft
>   inside locks of bone
> from where they'll never get out
> never in this world be free

I'll leave it all in the lake, Liz, let the ice close the hole, claim my failure, and turn it into folklore. I've given it plenty of material.

GOOD STUDENT, GOOD TEACHER

Take out a piece of paper and a pen. Write this down.

The introduction must include the thesis and preview the points for your reader. Yes, the thesis has to be in the beginning. No, you can't write it your own way. Your way is wrong. This isn't high school; we have a different set of demands here, specific academic expectations that you need to know in order to survive other classes. No, your father can't help you. No one can help you. Sum up all of your points in the conclusion without introducing new ideas. Never use I.

Don't talk when I'm talking. Get off your cellphone. You'll be marked absent today for not having your books. Stay awake. Are you taking notes? Why aren't you writing this down? There are no excused absences; it doesn't matter where you were all of last week. Don't show me the doctor's note, the death certificate, the letter from the Dean regarding your chronic depression, the bruises, the scars, the icy yawn in yourself that you fall into daily that's getting harder and harder to climb out of and one day you won't. I don't accept late papers. Why are you crying? Don't bring your life into this classroom. Your job, your boyfriend, your mother dying of cancer, your father who blames you, your friends, your heart, your passion, your soul do not exist here. Use a semicolon to separate two independent clauses.

Underline as you read. Define all words you don't know. Don't summarize what the author says. Analyze. Interpret. The author will give clues on how to locate the argument. I don't know why he doesn't come right out and say it. But he won't. Or he can't. But he wants you to search, because maybe he's lost. Search in the patterns, the figurative language, the tone and diction and rhetorical strategies. Look for him between the lines, but be careful: it can be a hellish, labyrinthine place, so hold hands as you navigate. Try using a highlighter.

Who looked up the word labyrinthine?

See me during office hours. You aren't passing. You aren't taking this class seriously. Your biggest problem is you're writing the way you speak, and you speak poorly. You need to think in English. Your syntax and diction are horrible. *Awk.* means Awkward. Your language is awkward. It hobbles, it falls, it fails, it drowns your ideas in the ocean of your words. When I read your papers, I feel the ocean's breeze, smell the fish and seaweed, and the drumbeat of ancient culture thumps my chest so I can't breathe or see or think straight. It's distracting. Just proofread closer. Learn proper English. There are only seven weeks of class left. You'd better start working harder if you want to pass. And watch your possessives.

Use textual evidence to support your ideas. Use the voice of an authority. Your father—yes, the one who kicked you out of the house—he's an authority. Your mother—so what if she's hairless and medicated—she's an authority also. Me, your professor, I am absolutely an authority. You are not. You are an eighteen-year-old freshman with nothing original or insightful to say. You have no voice. You need to find one.

You keep coming back. You keep trying. F after F hasn't broken your spirit. How can I get through to you? What will it take to break you? Where do you get this ability to retain your idealism, your hope? Read it aloud for the class. Put it on the board. We'll workshop it together; we'll circle the verbs and diagram the sentence. We'll—there's no time, the period is over. You should withdraw from the course.

Is there something you want to tell me about the last paper you handed in? It shows too much improvement. You couldn't have written it. We take plagiarism very seriously at this university. As your professor, I am obligated to report this matter to the Dean and to inform you of the penalties. You will fail this class; you will be put on academic probation, and this will be on your permanent transcript. Your father will disown you for good; you will have to tell your mother, as she writhes in pain in her hospital bed, why you were kicked out of school, yours the last words she hears. You will stop eating, sleeping; you will lose your part-time job and your friends and your boyfriend and your faith in God. When there's nothing left to lose, you will find yourself on the roof of your dorm with the wind whipping your hair as your friends and classmates scurry like ants below, rushing to the classes they're easily passing with the papers in their backpacks they easily wrote, and the moment you step off the ledge, the scream you hear will be your voice.

Dependent and independent clauses. Dangling modifiers. Fragments and fused sentences. Commas to separate coordinating adjectives and appositives and adjective clauses and parenthetical phrases. The ocean. Gerunds. Subject- verb and pronoun-antecedent agreement. The difference between who and whom. The difference between lie and lay. The difference between you and me. MLA guidelines. Departmental guidelines. Parallel structure. Prepositions and prepositional phrases. The past participle articles antecedent subordinate subjunctive possessive transitive comparative superlative if God exists.

Write this way and you'll get a good grade. Then you'll survive your other classes. You'll go far. You'll get a good job, make a lot of money, live in a big house, develop a focused relationship, get married, raise your kids without using I, support your family with evidence from the reading, work and work until you retire and your spouse dies, watch television in the dark, die forgotten and alone in the recliner, but no argument at your end. No new ideas in your conclusion.

THE NIGHTMARES OF
FINNEGAN GRAVES

Here lies Finnegan Graves, read the tombstone at the foot of the bed, where Finnegan himself paused, placed his hand to his bony chest, and heralded the rest from memory:

> "He died while sleeping
> but his dreams are still creeping;
> instead of a grave to lay down his head
> he'd rather a bed to dream of the dead—
> 'the deader the better,'
> he's always said."

Humming, Finnegan hung up his raven-feather robe in the closet, and Simon and Peter crashed out from behind his suits groaning and gnarling up their spectral faces.

"Not bad, you two," Finnegan said to the teenage brothers ghosting around his ankles. "Now, skedaddle, it's time for bed," and they vanished, leaving behind a trail of smoky chuckles.

Bedtime indeed! Finnegan's favorite part of the day. He sat on the tawny, soiled mattress musing over his collection of torture recordings, sing-songing their titles: *Botched Executions and Slow Electrocutions, Lions on Loins, Grizzlies on Groins, Carcinegeous Toxinegous Venom Infusions*. He chose something light and placed the record on the player, double-checking that the timer was set for 2:00 a.m. and the volume was still at 3. From his pajama pockets, he removed a feisty -mouse and a handful of black spiders, which he dropped and sprinkled in the bed before getting in with them. Once snug under the greasy sheets, he turned the TV on with the remote, pressed play and, with a smile, dozed off to old medical footage of lepers rotting away on a beautiful Pacific Island...

A jungle at twilight, mutation abounds—verdant brush slick with slimy life, a thick soggy carpet of moss sucking the feet, gargantuan trees struggling against strangling vines—but the wild is muted of sound. There's a presence felt, things watching from shadows. Then, sloshing and slishing, wet flesh finds motion. The lepers, they are coming for him! The brush is too dense to run, so he must stand and wait to be overtaken. Suddenly, the sky alights like a meteor flash, and the jungle awakens in a din of cries. He is given sight to the trees far above where the branches are clumped with soggy lepers howling and screaming the best they can without tongues. They are furious with Finnegan, their putrescent scowls and back-of-the-throat howls are thrown down at him along with something else. It's cold and wet on his neck, like refrigerated oatmeal. The lepers, like monkeys, are snowballing their rotten flesh at him. With each juicy handful raining down, Finnegan is happier, until his arms are raised, face exposed, inviting the foul weather.

Then, a sliver of bone pierces his neck—

He woke with a start, heaving and sweating and scanning the darkness for the howling lepers until he realized he was in his room, the noises coming from the record player. On his shoulder, the mouse was attached and nibbling. He swatted it, then lay back and closed his eyes to try to re-dream the scene. This time, he hoped to be buried alive by raining flesh—no, better still, he hoped he would become a tree-perched leper, hurling fists of his own meat while barking from the hole in his face.

Finnegan drifted back off to sleep, hopeful as a child.

Simon and Peter darted into the bedroom and lapped at Finnegan's face with their fog-wet vapors. Morning: the worst part of the day.

"*Day* is the worst part of the day," Finnegan corrected, then shooed the ghosts away.

This morning, Finnegan had a reading to give uptown to promote his new horror novel, *Finger Puppets*. He loathed readings and his fans even more, but what got him out of bed was the thought of repulsing the audience with the disgusting details from his book. He yawned and stretched his lank, knocking into the gigantic taxidermy bat that served as the bed's canopy, brushed the spiders from his body, then urinated into one of the six tin buckets he kept in the room. He went to the closet and fetched one of his 19th century suits, sniffed it, then frowned. "You guys can do better than that!" Finnegan called to the closet's ceiling, budded with bats.

He dressed, combed his inky hair slick without a mirror, using his fingers instead to feel the perfectly pink part slicing the center of his skull and, keeping to routine, he did not brush his teeth.

Famished, Finnegan went out into the lab-like kitchen, sooty brick countertops lined with purple-glowing jars of fetuses and organs. From the pantry, he took an IV bag, hooked it onto the wheeled rack, and stuffed the tube into his vein. Finnegan was finicky about food and obsessed with keeping his skeletal figure.

He pulled the IV rack along as he rushed past his caged creatures— snakes, lizards, tarantulas, rabid possums, and a dog-sized rat named Buck— and into the study to retrieve his book. He searched the shelves cluttered with his own titles and his writing desk, an ancient druid altar still stained with sacrificial virgin blood. *Finger Puppets* was nowhere, and he was running late.

"Simon! Peter!"

They sleeked in, sheepish grins. "Yes?" they said in sync.

"I have no time for games," Finnegan said, knocking down the IV rack. "I will put you two in the ghost pound if that book doesn't appear in my hand immediately."

Luckily for Finnegan, Simon and Peter were marvelously gullible. The absurd threat never failed, and the book was produced.

"Thank you."

Finnegan snatched his keys and raced for the door, nearly tripping over Theresa's mutilated body—a wax corpse—on his way out.

This is the life of Finnegan Graves. However, it's about to change. "It is?" he said, poking his head out of the closing elevator doors. It is.

Two hours later, Finnegan was returning from the reading when he noticed down the hall a little Chinese girl and her mother moving boxes into the apartment across from his. Up until that moment, he had been giddy since he had managed to elicit vomit and tears from the audience, then clear the entire auditorium, in only two paragraphs. Therefore, he didn't have to autograph anyone's book and had been hoping to avoid human contact altogether that day. His luck had run out.

He was already halfway down the hall and was sure the little girl had spotted him, so he couldn't turn back around. Instead, he pulled his keys from his pocket and pretended to fiddle with them as he continued. He kept his keys strung on the limp tail of a dead mouse, and Finnegan displayed its gray, decaying carcass as he moved past the girl to try to ward her off. When he got to the door, he could see her staring. There was suddenly a clamor of Chinese prattle, apparently from the mother, which so startled Finnegan that he fumbled his keys. When he stooped to retrieve them, they were snatched by a crafty hand.

He heard from behind, "Here you go Mister."

Finnegan turned to find the little girl, maybe eight or nine, smiling under her red baseball cap, holding up his dead mouse and keys in her small palm. She was cute: green eyes that twinkled, plump cheeks that dimpled, a gap in her tiny teeth from where her tiny tongue liked to peek. Finnegan was nauseated by her adorable face and the cute rhyme used to describe it.

While the little girl stood quietly, hand still raised in offering, her mother was a bluster of commotion, wrestling packages and bags, chattering vehemently to no one in particular. The mother then noticed Finnegan standing there, staring, and she said, "Oh, hello to you," then continued right on with her solipsistic business. Finnegan looked back down to the girl who had remained fixed in her position.

He found himself dumb at her offering, until she spoke. "What are you afraid of ?" she lisped in perfectly precious English. "Don't you want these?"

This snapped Finnegan out of his trance; he snatched his keys, snarled at the girl, and swirled around to unlock his door. Before going in, he heard a giggle and a "Have a nice day!" Finnegan slammed the door so hard his bones shook.

For the rest of the afternoon, he was cranky, *What are you afraid of ?* echoing in his skull. His first thought was to murder her, maybe lacing a cupcake with strychnine and leaving it at her front door or setting a booby-trap of some sort, a kind of rusty jaw contraption that would clamp mother and daughter both. Finnegan sat at his stone desk and wrote out the details of this trap. He even doodled sketches of it with its slinky springs and sinister teeth, clogs and levers, pulleys and rings—a kind of perpetual motion machine. This calmed him considerably, and then he laughed—actually croaked a laugh—at getting so flustered. In this rare, jovial mood, he decided to feed Buck, whom he had been starving to pit against the other creatures for a battle royale. His favorite pet deserved a meal. He put a skillet on the hot stove and filled it with lard, grabbed a handful of live beetles from a barrel in the pantry, and sprinkled them into the screaming hot grease. From one of the many jars of pickled oddities, he hoisted out what appeared to be a small intestine. He chopped this in chunks and dropped them into the mix. Listening to the beetles fry and intestine snap, sniffing the stench, and then feeding Buck the gruel, made Finnegan sleepy with pleasure. Even though it was only 9 p.m., Finnegan set up his record player, got into bed, watched some torture footage, then fell asleep.

When dawn came, Finnegan was found sitting in the electric chair in the shadowy corner of the bedroom, arms folded and scowling. He'd had a dream that night, a dream of *her*, of that awful girl. It was just a peek, a fleeting glimpse of her like a comet racing through his nightmare. But it was... nice. It was sunshine and rainbows and unicorns nice. He was having a fine old nightmare of being boiled alive in oil, a giant beetle coming along and pecking pieces of his head with its pincers. And then—flash!— there she was, her face pure and bright, holding in her hand a yellow songbird, the most disgusting, awful, nasty—most beautiful yellow he had ever seen. When he woke, he tried to conjure images of the songbird pecking her to death so that when he fell back asleep, he could enjoy this dream, but he couldn't sleep. He couldn't get that color stain out of the black fabric of his mind, so he sat on his electric chair and pouted the rest of the night. And plotted his revenge.

He stood at the door with his bloodshot eye sliming the peephole, waiting for the brat. Little girls hate snakes and rats, he gleefully thought as he estimated the weight of the fat boa around his neck and squeezed fidgety Buck in his hands. He wasn't going to release them on the girl or her mother; he would simply wait for them to come out, then pretend he was just leaving, and follow them into the elevator while both—particularly the girl—squealed in terror. He would then bottle up her fright for nocturnal savoring.

Their door swung open, and out clattered the mother, followed by the happy little girl. Finnegan rushed for the doorknob but realized he had both hands on Buck, and two were barely enough. He now wished he hadn't forbidden Simon and Peter from joining the prank. He panicked, his opportunity slipping away, so he quickly borrowed one of his hands for the knob and jerked the door open. In doing so, Buck went wild, and Finnegan stumbled out into the hall, trying to get a handle on the rat, the boa tensing up, the mother and girl looking on. Finnegan had to drop Buck to keep the boa from strangling him, and the rat turned on its master—perhaps in revenge for last night's meal—and attacked his calf. Finnegan yelped, the boa tightened, and the mother spouted off some angry Chinese. The girl, however, assumed a kicker's stance, took three prancing steps toward Finnegan and, with perfect, graceful form, punted Buck off his calf, sending the rat flying nearly twenty feet down the hall, to land motionless in a heap of fur. She then reached up and cupped the snake's head in her tiny hands and shushed it with a sibilant song. Immediately, Finnegan felt the tubular muscle loosen, and his sight and breathing returned.

What followed was a cobwebby shame made only bearable by the fiery pain in his calf. The mother was still chattering, seemingly annoyed at some entirely different situation. The girl was crouched at Finnegan's foot, inspecting the blood trickling onto his leather wingtip shoe.

"You sure know how to make an entrance," the girl said, looking up at Finnegan and, by God, winking.

He was about to spit in her face when the mother rushed at him, shouting, "You! Take my Helen. I'll be back dinnertime or so. Go ahead, take her."

"Me take? You're handing your child off to me? I could be a...serial killer."

"You're not a killer. You're a circus clown."

Finnegan was about to protest when he remembered the enormous snake hugging his shoulders.

The mother turned to her daughter. "Go on with circus clown." Her eyes steadied on Finnegan a moment, and she pressed herself closer to the girl, sneaking her something from her purse. "Just in case."

"I don't need this," the girl laughed, and Finnegan spied a butcher knife being pushed back down to its hiding place. "I'll be fine."

The mother shrugged and scurried away down the hall, stepping over Buck's corpse.

"What do you mean, *fine?*" Finnegan shouted at the girl. "I'm not babysitting you…. I won't stand for this…. I—"

"Is that a dead body?" the girl marveled, moving inside Finnegan's apartment.

"Don't—stop—get back here." But she had already gone in. Finnegan followed, wincing at his Buck-bite, hefting the now unwieldy snake. The girl was on her knees inspecting Theresa's wax wounds, uttering "Cool" at every detail. He wished he could toss her out cartoon style until he considered an even better strategy, one that might accomplish his initial goal.

Finnegan put down the snake, appropriated the air of a sinister count, and paced behind her, saying, "I'd have you know, little girl, that's real." He then crouched and croaked in her ear, "I killed her myself just this morning."

The girl laughed. "Yeah, right. I'm not stupid." She examined the detail of the missing jaw. "But it sure looks real." She stood, nearly crashing into Finnegan's chin. "This place is like the coolest Halloween haunted house, ever!"

Unfazed, Finnegan asked, "Want to see more?"

"Yeah," she whispered.

"Follow me then," Finnegan lured. To add to his character, he pulled up some blood from his wound and licked it, noting the taste with an *mmmm*.

"You should probably get a rabies shot for that," the girl said.

Finnegan told her to shut up.

To enter his apartment, they had to pass through a narrow hall lit with small red lights only bright enough to illuminate Finnegan's photo collection of various oddities: accidents, crime-scene stills, and a whole slew of medical anomalies including 50-pound tumors and birth defects. Finnegan urged the girl to take a look. She did, but in fascination, and she actually stopped at his favorite, Siamese twins with elephantitis. Finnegan stepped closer to her. "They're friends of mine. They might be coming over soon for lunch."

Just then, Simon and Peter, sniffing out a little attention, began show-ing off. The pictures spun on the wall, the lights flickered, and an icy wind came blowing through. The girl stood silent, holding her cap on her head, watching the spectacle until it ended a minute later. Then she slowly craned her head up to Finnegan, eyes wide, mouth parted. Finnegan licked his rotting teeth in anticipation of her scream, but instead he got an, "Oh my God, that was so cool! You actually have ghosts here?" and she trotted down the hall saying, "What else do you have in this place?"

Finnegan kicked the wall with his bad leg and yelped.

The rest of the afternoon faired no better for Finnegan's cause. This cute little girl was fascinated with all of his most prized possessions: the caged creatures and bottled-creepies, the bat bed and electric chair. Other things that displeased her she dismissed as ridiculous. She commented that his buckets of urine were unsanitary; that "bat poop" would ruin the fabric of his priceless suits; and when Finnegan, getting desperate, removed a pickled foot from the jar, bit off the pinky toe, and chewed it very delib-erately (mainly to keep from gagging), she said, "That will make you sick," and turned to inspect something else.

At one point, she asked about the hidden door in the dingiest, dust-iest, cobwebbiest nook of the apartment, the one with a massive padlock securing the knob. "Is that a dungeon where you keep prisoners chained to the walls?"

"No, that's nothing. Get out of there," Finnegan faltered, then tried to recover. "I mean, yes, that's where I keep little girls, but I'm... renovating. Now, come on."

By day's end, they were in the bedroom watching film of surgical experimentation on concentration campers, the girl lying on her stomach on the bed, her head in her hands, kicking her feet, Simon and Peter on each side of her mirroring her posture, and Finnegan sitting in the electric chair, defeated and grouchy. When the doorbell rang, the girl popped up and said, "Well, gotta go," and, "Thanks for the awesome day." Finnegan just sat there, pouting.

"Hey," the girl came back in the room. "Don't you want to know my name?"

"No," Finnegan grunted.

"Well, I want to know yours."

"Go to hell."

The girl laughed, "You're funny." Then she said, "My name is Helen," and slipped her little warm hand into Finnegan's and squeaked, "Pleased to meet you." Finnegan pulled his hand away and turned his head. She skipped off, singing her goodbyes: "Goodbye, giant bat; goodbye, baby-in-a-jar; goodbye, snakes-n-things; goodbye, bumpy twins; goodbye, ghosts;" and then, faintly, "Hello, Mama."

There's something in the shadows, a hulky creature fat and feral. When it moves, its bloated belly scrapes the stone floor, an angry grunt evidence of its effort. The clickety-clack clamor of its teeth clashes against bone until, from the shadows, a long, clean tibia flies and clackety-clicks at Finnegan's feet. Or foot. He looks down his torso and sees that one leg has been gnawed off at the knee. He is chained to the wall, and what is in the shadow wants more. It grunts as it hefts its hulk out of the dark, and Finnegan is aghast.

It is Buck, but not the Buck he expects. This is a Disney version of his once-menacing rat: huge, happy eyes pooled with glistening pupils; plump, rosy cheeks adorned with wavy whiskers; a triangular sniffer twitching about his face; and a wide smile revealing a candy-red tongue and two pearly chompers. His round body is coated with fluffy fur, and twirling about his rear is a pink, bubble-gum tail. What's worse, as he prances about the dungeon, his path cartoons into a vibrant green meadow and shimmering pond with cattails and bullfrogs and, rising up from the lush, a hundred yellow songbirds fill the sky, move off into the horizon, then ribbon back around, toward Finnegan, closer and closer, until they shroud him in their song and in that impossible hue.

Finnegan opened his eyes, still drifting in the bliss. As he came to his senses, he worked to blink the yellow out and the grays and blacks back in. When his vision was sufficiently achromatic again, he spanked and kicked the mattress until he was out of breath, at which point he simply lay, huffing.

What got him out of bed was a motivation to write. Finnegan sat at his desk, pushed aside his other project, and picked up his phalange pen to put to paper a description of how one might destroy a little girl so that it lasted years. He got no further than the phrase: 'First, you take her pigtails,' when the doorbell rang.

Finnegan slammed down his pen, snapping the bone in two, and stomped to the door. When he opened it, nobody was there. Then he looked down and saw Buck's body stuffed inside a strangely decorated shoe box. He picked it up by its handle for closer inspection and saw it was a handmade coffin. The outside of the box was adorned with 20-30 living cockroaches pasted on, their little legs still kicking. At this point, Finnegan realized the handle he was holding was actually Buck's severed tail stapled to the box. Buck himself was blanketed in black-painted flower petals, and his eyes had been plucked out and replaced with yellow jellybeans. There was a note inside: *Sorry for killing your pet, and I hope this is a good place for it to be dead.—Helen.* The case of the missing eyeballs was solved in the word 'good.' Finnegan examined the craftsmanship of the box, trying to hide his admiration since the girl was probably watching through the door hole. Unsettled by the thought, he retreated into his lair and closed the door.

Inside, he set the coffin on the dining room table and stepped back to appreciate the maze of movement from the cockroach legs. Finnegan had been sent many gifts by his fans, typically insipid things they assumed he'd appreciate, like cow tongues or animal bones or fuzzy photos of ghosts, but he had never been given something that he genuinely appreciated for its attention to the macabre. However difficult it was to abandon his abhorrence of the girl, he realized it was in his better interest to find out more about her.

"That's a good way to put it: 'my better interest.'"

Who was she? Where did she come from? Most importantly: Why could she not scare? He wasn't going to soften his heart to her.

"No way!"

And he definitely wouldn't forgive her for invading his dreams.

"Not a chance."

Finnegan decided there was nothing wrong with finding out a little more information.

"Nothing wrong with information."

Finnegan dressed and polished his face and raked his hair oil-slick and didn't brush his teeth. On his way to the door, he paused over a styrofoam head modeling the floppy skin-mask of a notorious Russian sociopath. It probably wouldn't have an effect, but he grabbed it anyway, positioned it on his face, and walked out across the hall. He raised his skull-white fist, held it for a beat, two beats, *three*, then finally brought it down on the door. There was nothing, then there was muffled commotion, and Finnegan felt silly waiting there, masked like a tricker-treater. He was about to remove the face when the girl opened the door out of breath, her hat lopsided on her head, hair oddly off-kilter. Caught mid de-masking, Finnegan looked through the eyeholes and said the first thing that came to mind: "Boo." The girl laughed, and he chuckled and removed it.

"Is that real person skin?" she asked.

"Yes, from a Russian murderer named Vlad the Butcher."

"Can I try it?"

Finnegan cocked his head as if not hearing her right, but her gimmee hands confirmed the request. He handed over the mask, and she eagerly covered her delicate face with the leathery gore. With one hand keeping it in place and the other holding an imaginary knife, Helen cutely imitated a Russian accent, saying, "I am murderer. Vlad will cut you up." She brought the phantom knife down on Finnegan, who found it all delightful. The girl removed the mask, and both shared a laugh.

"Do you want to come inside?" she asked.

"Oh, well, I just came to—" Finnegan peered over her shoulder.

"My mother is out if that's what you're scared of."

"I'm not scared!" he snapped, casting off his uncertainty and walking inside her apartment. The place was disgustingly homey, with drapes that matched the couches and couches that matched the drapes, end tables with lamps and ceramic knick-knacks, framed paintings of flowers and oceans, and scented candles smelling of flowers and oceans. Finnegan was shamefully aware of his bat fragrance.

"It's a little different from yours," the girl acknowledged, still catching her breath.

Finnegan didn't know where to put himself—the closet would probably be best, but he didn't want to appear vulnerable, so he leaned his back against the taupe wall and folded his arms as if this place were made for him. Helen fluttered to every switch in the apartment, flicking off lights, then pulled the drapes closed. The result was a much darker—and calmer—ambiance. The girl then walked to the wall next to Finnegan and sat on the floor, hugging her knees. Finnegan did the same.

"You got the coffin I made?"

"Oh, yes," Finnegan perked, then abated his enthusiasm, shrugging awkwardly.

"It took me all night to find the cockroaches and glue them on."

A few wispy sounds from the busy street stories below the window ghosted between them.

"Didn't it bother you?" Finnegan asked.

"What?"

Finnegan nervously picked out some type of flesh from below his long fingernails.

"The cockroaches, plucking out the eyes, cutting off the tail, that kind of thing?"

"Why would it?" Her expression conveyed honesty.

"Because you're a little girl. Girls your age should be scared of those things."

This remark appeared to affect Helen. "Oh," she said, looking forward. Then she whipped her head back, "Well, I'm not."

"That's exactly what I'm curious about," Finnegan said, adjusting his sitting position to relieve the pressure from his tailbone. "Why aren't you scared? Anyone, even adults, would have been frightened by me, by my creatures, the ghosts, the pictures and movies and things in the jars. There wasn't one single thing that scared you. Why not?"

To this, Helen answered quickly, with a squinty look that said this was a silly question. "Because all that stuff's fake."

Finnegan thought he had her and sat up. "But it's not. The ghosts are real—they're not a trick. The photos on the walls are of real people with real deformities. Those things I have in jars—"

"I mean it's fake to me because there's realer stuff to be afraid of. Only real stuff scares me."

Finnegan didn't like that at all. He stared the girl down, thought of giving her something real to be afraid of.

"And you know what?" she continued without flinching. "That stuff's not real to you either."

Finnegan gave her sweet face a sinister glare, then got up.

"You don't know what you're talking about. You're just a girl." And he marched away.

"I'm sorry," she said, getting up and walking after him. "I didn't mean to make you mad."

"Oh, shut up," he growled, jerking open the door and slamming it behind him. He paused in the hallway between Helen's door and his, heaving, fisting his hands to disguise their shaking. He noticed mail wedged into the door slot, which he yanked out and, simply as a distraction, rifled through. He moaned when he came to a postcard from Antarctica.

When Finnegan was a boy, he used to scavenge for dead things and, like a cat, bring them home to his mother as gifts. Throughout his childhood, his mother would have found placed at her feet: spiders, frogs, lizards, snakes, mice, birds, squirrels, and, at times, cats. His mother cherished her little Finn and his offerings, rewarding him with a tender kiss on the nose and some hot cocoa.

His father, on the other hand, was a miserable man. He would come home from work in his second-hand suit, shoulders slavery-slouched, sit down at the dinner table ignoring both son and wife, and scoop food into his mouth without savor. Then he would get up from the table and go to bed. On weekends when he didn't work, he didn't get out of bed.

One evening, they were all sitting at the dinner table, sawing and gnawing at their meal of liver and beats. For some forgotten reason, Finn wanted to include his father on his scavenging stories, wanted to know what he did at work, but mainly wanted to cheer his father up. Finn lowered his head to try to catch his gaze, but his mother saw what he was up to and pinched his knee under the table. Finn ignored her and persisted until, finally, his father looked at him. It was at that moment that he realized his colossal mistake, for little Finn was stuck staring into the eyes of a nightmare. The eyelids were mouths that sucked at gummy sacks, eyeballs like amphibian eggs—translucent, slimy, sightless. They seemed to be eyes that had overseen and quit long ago, left to rot in the sockets. These eyes could no longer recognize good. These eyes were the windows into hell, and little Finn had a prime view.

When his father finally dropped his head back down to his meal, Finn gasped relief and stuffed a hunk of liver into his mouth to put his nerves to use. However, not one minute later, Finn's father placed his silverware soundlessly on his plate, pushed his chair out, and removed himself from the table. He then went into the bathroom and shot himself.

Almost immediately after the gunfire, his mother told Finn with a smile, "Finish your dinner, sweetie. I'll be right back." She went into the linen closet and hoisted an armful of towels into the bathroom, then a bucket, mop, and cleaner. Sloppy mop sounds and humming traveled into the kitchen. Periodically, she would come out to check on Finn, a smile plastered on her face, specks of blood on her sleeves.

"Almost ready for bed, baby?"

Finn was lost. He hadn't moved. There was still a mound of half- masticated liver on his tongue.

His mother walked him down the hall, past the bathroom with the door closed. In bed, Finn heard more cleaning, whistling meant for his ears and, late into the night, he thought there might have been red flashing lights splashing on his wall, murmurings of men. It could have been a dream. It all could have been a dream.

In the morning, Finn woke badly needing to urinate, but he dared not use the bathroom. So he rummaged his closet for the blue plastic bucket he kept his crayons in and, without even dumping the contents, relieved himself into it. He then hid the bucket back in the closet and, cautiously, opened his bedroom door. Down the hall, his mother was sitting at the kitchen table. She perked and trotted to meet him with a big smile, kissing his face and fixing his bed hair.

"Do you need to use the bathroom, sweetie?" she chirped.

"No, thank you."

"You sure?" She stood and twirled and opened the bathroom door like a gameshow girl revealing the prize. Finn didn't want to speak. "There's nothing to be afraid of, baby," and she put her hand on his back and pushed him into the threshold of the bathroom. "See?" Every surface and tile and rim sparkled, and the scent of bleach was biting. The cleanliness was as conspicuous as what had been cleaned, and Finn wanted out at once.

"I'm hungry, Mama."

"Good! I have breakfast waiting," she relinquished him and led the way to the kitchen, "and something to show you."

On the kitchen table was a stack of pancakes, a plate of breakfast meats, and a note. "It's from your father," his mother said cheerfully. "He had to leave early this morning and wanted me to be sure you got this." She pulled the chair out and escorted him to it, then opened the note and handed it to Finn. "He wanted me to be sure you got this. He told me himself."

Finn's hands shook as he took the yellow-lined paper with the familiar script. It said this:

Finn,

I regret that I have to leave you before saying good-bi. But work gave me a very important mission that I can't turn down. I am going to Antarctica to study penguins. There are a lot of penguins down there and I have to study all of them so I will probably be there for a very long time. However I will send you postcards often and your mother who loves you beyond words will devote herself to taking care of you.

Your a good boy Finn. Theres no need to be afraid.

Love,
Your Father

As promised, Finnegan had received postcards from Antarctica for the past 30 years. They always depicted penguins, but the post office stamp always read Ohio, and the handwriting was always the same loopy scroll as his list of after-school chores. That she never bothered to disguise her script but took pains to fake everything else always compelled Finnegan to shred these postcards and discard them in his piss buckets. Except today. He went into his apartment, turned the postcard over as if it were a Tarot card revealing his fate, and read: *I miss you Finn. Hope your being good to your mother. You should call her today. Your my brave boy. Love Your father.*

Finnegan squeezed the postcard in his fist in direct proportion to his face squeezing his eyes and mouth together. Something was building and flaming, and he was fighting it hard. *Goddamn you, Finnegan, you stupid baby.*

In his ribs—in his clunky parts—there was a clicking and a cranking, axles grinding, the works of a clock unworking, a malfunctioning. An explosion.

Finnegan threw himself against the wall, smashing the plaster and maybe snapping a bone; he trampled Theresa, murdering her for real this time; raged down the hall, swiping the pictures off along the way. He charged for the creatures, all of them frightened for their lives; he crashed the glass, tore open the cages, and stomped them to death. In the kitchen, he hurled the jars, the scummy contents sliming across the floor and into the bedroom. There, he toppled the giant bat, heaved the tombstone over his head, and brought it down on his record collection.

When the physical was ransacked and Finnegan stood heaving in the mess, Simon and Peter scurried for a place to hide. He did not seek them out; rather, he went for a different ghost. Still stuck in a craze, Finnegan devolved to his hands and knees and crawled into the back of his closet, then reversed, dragging a trunk. He raised the creaky lid, which suddenly sobered him. He took a deep breath, then plunged his hand into the intestines of the trunk and pulled out one of its undigested contents: a very cold, very heavy, very real revolver. He discovered it years ago in the attic of his childhood home when he helped his mother move and kept it as evidence of reality. As he turned it around in his twiggy hands, he thought, Little Helen was right: this was the only frightening artifact he possessed.

But he was not afraid.

"I'm not afraid," Finnegan repeated.

But evidence was needed.

Finnegan stood and walked to the cobwebby, padlocked bathroom door, the weighty gun hanging like a pendulum at the end of his arm. He knew one day his path would lead him here. The image of himself standing before the door was very familiar, as if it were a scene from a book he wrote. That may have been why he kept the key conveniently placed above the door. He retrieved it, maneuvered it into the rusty padlock, and turned it until he felt the pop. He loosed the lock from the knob and pushed the door open and flicked on the light. Cockroaches scattered into cracks, leaving their leggy punctuations in the dust. They were a comfort—the mirror over the sink was not. It was his fate and, as if proving that fact to Finnegan, the mirror was perfectly polished. Finnegan stepped before it, keeping only to his copy's chest. He will have to raise his eyes.

He is not afraid.

"I am not afraid," he said.

He'll use the gun as a focus, follow it up to his head, and there, the eyes. He did this, the muzzle on his temple like a snake's icy, puckered kiss, but the eyes did not obey. They tarried at his chest, at the knot of his brown tie pulsing by the heart's sparrow flutter. He squeezed his eyes shut, seeing flashes from the blood rocking his temples, then opened them on themselves: swollen, yellowed eyeballs, wolf-green irises, pin-pricks of pupil, thin brow framing a nasty, mean stare. A man in a bathroom mirror glaring himself down with a gun to his brain—Who was this, Finnegan or Father? It didn't matter; the one on this side hated both.

He pulled the trigger.

The body collapsed on the vanity, the opened-up head steaming the mirror. The brains exposed in the reflection revealed a backwards thought zipping between synapses in electric-current cursive: *diarfa ton ma I*. Then it flickered out. On this side of the mirror, Finnegan still stood, holding the revolver to his head, looking at his corpse with a forwardly thought: *Why am I still alive?*

—Because, there's a different epitaph yet to be carved into Finnegan's granite plan, one that waits across the hall, one he will not like.

"I won't?" No, Finnegan.

"Will you come with me?"

Only part of the way.

Shaking, Finnegan set the gun down, and we walked together through the ravaged apartment. He paused at the door. He had his hands in his pockets. He was looking at the floor.

I'm not going to open it for you.

He was about to call for Simon and Peter, somewhere still in hiding.

You have to do it yourself.

He grumbled, put his hand on the knob, exhaled, then opened the door.

Across the hall, Helen's mother was crying in the doorway of her apartment. She saw Finnegan but continued weeping. Finnegan stepped into the hall to view beyond her. Men were backing out of the apartment, pulling something. As they neared, one man looked over his shoulder and said, "Could you step aside, ma'am, sir?"

Both did, and the medics emerged with a short gurney, a white sheet draped over a tiny body. As it was wheeled past, Finnegan noticed the small, bald crown of a head peeking from the sheet, which gave him a moment's relief. However, the medics offered something to the mother, parking the gurney just beside Finnegan. The white sheet shrouded the features of a child's face, sunken at the eyeholes and gaping mouth—a ghost glaring at him. Finnegan looked away.

The mother had refused whatever was offered her, so the medic tried Finnegan. He dumbly accepted as the medics resumed pushing the gurney down the hall and out of sight.

"She's better off now," the mother choked out. "No more suffering now." Then she burst into another fit of tears and fled into her apartment, leaving Finnegan dazed in the hall. It was then that he acknowledged what he held in his hands. He yelped and dropped it; he wiped his hands on his pants, and he backed away from it until he crashed against his door. He couldn't turn his back on it, so he sneaked his hand behind him to turn the knob. It wouldn't turn. He tried harder—it was stuck or locked. He swore the thing was inching towards him. He kicked at the door with his heel, tried crying out, but his throat was bone dry. It was a costume, a cover-up; it was a mask, a lie. Finally, the knob loosed, and he crashed in, then slammed and locked the door on what lay limp on the floor: a shiny black wig attached to a red ballcap.

Here lies Finnegan Graves,
Sleeping as soundly as the dead
until he bolts upright in bed
to the sounds of a poor soul screaming,
but it's from him the screams are streaming.
He balls himself up against the headboard;
there's no light to turn on, no mother to beg for.
   Finnegan Graves is afraid—
   "I'm afraid," to the dark he says.

WORD MADE FLESH

I. Congregation

And the men came down the mountain, came out the wilderness cast in furs and skins, the smart of beast and rot and rank on their gnarled bodies, a fearful mystery in their eyes. In the damp early morning, the waiting multitude gasped and backstepped to the lip of the sea, crisp at their heels. Women and children and men, they locked arms and shivered, but not from the cold. From the mountain, men charged forth, one of them, fanged and noseless and translucent-eyed. He spoke, and when he spoke, the creatures of the mount spewed from his mouth. These bobcats these wolves these deer these snakes these squirrels these scorpions these bats these beetles these owls these all shrouded the multitude in a deafening cloud. When it was all told, the savage teller reclaimed the creatures into his mouth, and the men retreated back into the wilderness and up the mountain, leaving the sea to lap at the congregation of bones.

II. Summoning

Mark wakes to a song that is not the heron's, not the crane's, the clapper rail's, the toad's, the sea's—though, for a moment, before fully awake, the human voices harmonize with these. Then they wrench themselves apart, each sound separate. He sits up in the cordgrass, stomps at a fiddler crab to scoot it away. The sweltering morning air already presses on him. Mark doesn't know how he slept, if he did. The kind of alert, fidgety sleep that doesn't count as far as the body is concerned. He rocks and sways as if on a boat, though he's still. It takes two attempts to brush the beetles from his legs. His tongue feels like a sandy slug in his mouth. The singing compels him. He crawls toward it, peeks through the grass.

A group of ten men and women sing at the water on the lawn of the white, paint-flaked church. The men's collared shirts cling to their backs, sweat-speckled. A larger man's shorts are darkly ringed in the crotch. The women's hair frizzes in the humidity, and their faces glisten. They begin with hymns Mark's never heard before. The shift is almost indiscernible as they retreat into their own prayer, their own world. They wander to their solitary part of the shore, where the lawn becomes marshy cordgrass, and they call at the sea. Go back. Go back. Soon, the English breaks apart, crippled into gibberish. Now the parishioners are frenzied, shouting, spinning, many knee-deep in the water, scooping armfuls over their heads. A small, sinewy woman grabs hold of the grass and leans impossibly forward, angled acutely towards the horizon. She weeps painfully, popping neck veins.

Breaking the surface near the shore—a boy. He is shirtless and all rib-cage, dark haired. He comes up out of the water, pulling a chain-linked basket. He walks just past the leaning-lady, who does not notice him. Nobody notices. The boy crouches on the church lawn and plucks oysters out of the dredges. His sharp knees catch the sun like headlights. He pulls a hatchet from the beltloop of his cut-offs and hacks apart the clumped oysters. He looks in Mark's direction. Mark collapses to his stomach, bent stalks jabbing his ribs. He tries to hide, but the boy is coming.

III. The Secret in the Bone

The boy offers Mark the shimmering, pink oyster. Its juices brim over the shell.

You need this, the boy says.

Mark doesn't know if he should abide the boy, for many reasons. Still, he is famished and thirsty. He takes the oyster, the juice running down his trembling hands. He tips it into his mouth, the sharp shell nipping his upper lip. His tongue becomes alive again, awakened by the oyster's silk and the ocean's tang. His throat is quenched and coated. Mark hears himself hum. The boy sits in the grass and picks up another oyster rock. He uses a knife to pry it open, then loosen the meat's muscle. He offers it to Mark who sucks it down.

You need to go home now, the boy says. Or eat. Even then, you need to go.

Again, Mark doesn't know if he should acknowledge him. The sounds of wildlife return.

The parishioners have quit; each is bent over or on a knee, gasping, sweating, fisting the ground.

There's no home, Mark croaks.

The boy splits another oyster. Mark's body tingles with want, and it takes effort to shake his head. He tucks his hands into his armpits to control their violent trembling.

The boy slurps the oyster, then wipes his mouth with the length of his arm. He stands and turns, makes the smallest gesture with his hand that commands Mark. When Mark gets to his feet, he wobbles, rainbow static splotching his vision. He stumbles through the high, stiff grass after the boy.

Once his feet find the church lawn, Mark sees the parishioners laid out on the ground, their limbs contorted like collapsed dummies. This looks like a battleground after fresh retreat, but there is no specter of violence, just bodies left as if abandoned.

The boy steps over a fleshy white woman, her eyes clear and squintless peering at the sun. Beetles swarm her body, paying special attention to the mouth.

Mark feels a tug. It's the boy, pulling him toward the shore. His small hand is mighty. Mark instantly finds himself ankle-deep in the warm sea.

I can teach you to oyster, the boy says. A man can live his whole life eating nothing but.

Mark's toes dig into the mushy bottom. Shell grit gets under the nails. He feels a larger man's weight pressing into him, straining entirely on his knees.

Or, the boy says, I can teach you to die.

Mark nods, the tremors in his hands moving up his chest, his throat, bouncing his chin.

The boy puts his hand to Mark's back and points to the water. He says, They'll be coming soon. When they do, offer yourself, and listen closely to how you're consumed. Pay attention to the bone. The secret's there.

THE BALLAD OF GUERRY JOHNS

John Henry went to the section boss,
Says the section boss what kin you do?
Says I kin line a track, I kin histe a jack,
I kin pick and shovel too,
I kin pick and shovel too.

I.

The night Guerry Johns was born, double forks of lightning knifed the skies over Northern New Jersey, and the Passaic River momentarily shifted directions, but nobody would notice. The latest news development distracted them; this time a dirty bomb had gone off in a New York City subway, leaving fifty people dead.

When the doctor held newborn Guerry up, glistening and squirmy, Mama Johns and the nurses gasped at the double-size of his arms and hands, thick and strong like an adult dwarf's. Later, the doctor came into Mama Johns's room with an X-ray. He explained, with one ear on the news calling from the mounted TV, that Guerry was born with two sets of bones and muscles in each arm and each hand. The humeri, radii, and ulnae stacked one on top of the other, along with double sets of carpals, metacarpals, and phalanges.

"Never seen or heard anything like it," the doctor spoke at the TV. He sighed, then said with forced interest to Mama Johns, "You won't have more children. He did a number on your uterus with those arms."

"Those hammers gonna be the death of me," she slurred due to the painkillers. Then she looked at the shaky, televised images of smoke and police, "How this world gonna take my boy?"

Guerry graduated from high school, and Mama Johns took him out to an Italian restaurant to celebrate. When their meals came, she said, "Got to go out and find some work."

As Guerry cut into his osso buco, the plate beneath snapped in two, and his collared shirt ripped at the shoulders. He threw down his silverware.

"Mama, there's nothing I can do with these impediments."

"You got arms like sledgehammers. Got to be some use for you somewhere." Mama stuffed a meatball into her mouth, then said around it, "Good ol' fashion gruntwork is what you need."

The next morning, Mama Johns pinned a list of employers on the sleeve of Guerry's sweatshirt. He got on the bus, knocking dents into handrails on his way to a seat. His first stop was an unloading dock way out in Bayonne where, last night, Mama spoke of dockhands loading and unloading cargo. Guerry visited the manager in his office, a man with a clean white shirt and tie, who marveled at Guerry's arms. He then walked Guerry out onto the dock and pointed to the cranes and mechanical arms hauling large crates in and out of ships. "Have any experience operating those?" the manager asked.

"No sir," Guerry said, and the manager shrugged and returned to his office.

Instead of finding big men swinging hammers at the Watchung quarry, as Mama Johns promised, Guerry found similar machinery working the rock. The nearby lumberyard imported its logs rather than hiring men to chop trees, and a giant, computerized saw shaped the wood. He trekked out to the Morristown and Erie railroad, and when Guerry asked if there was a need for a man to drive railroad spikes, the manager doubled over in laughter. A few contractors might have hired Guerry at the various construction sites if it hadn't been for the long line of men and women looking for work. They were all more skilled with nail guns and jigsaws.

"Got to get you on disability," Mama Johns said that night in the living room as they watched the news. "No one can deny those arms gettin' in your way of a salary."

Mama filled out the paperwork for Guerry. The day his disability came through, she fixed a nice dinner of fried porkchops, mashed potatoes and gravy, and corn on the cob. She took a twenty from her sock and gave it to Guerry to pick up some cold beers down the road. They both got tipsy during the meal as she told stories of growing up in North Carolina.

Mama Johns stumbled on the stairs trying to go up to bed. Guerry carried her to her room.

Guerry didn't smell coffee when he woke in the morning or hear Mama's slippers shuffling the tile floor of the kitchen. He called for her, then went into her bedroom. She was wheezing, chest bounding for breaths, and a grimace cut her face in half. "I'm dying, boy," she whispered as Guerry neared. "Those hammers, Lord, those hammers."

Guerry whined, grabbed up Mama's hands in his, and cried into her bosom. The birdy bones of her hands snapped at his grip.

"Guerry boy," she told, "you gotta let your mama go."

"No ma'am," he said. His tears iced his knuckles. Mama's hands continued to crunch in his.

"Son," Mama whispered, "got to let me go."

A violent tremble rattled Guerry and he whined, hardly able to speak. "What's the point of these hands, Mama?"

"Holdin' on to me ain't it." She lifted her head an inch. "Now mind your mama, and do as you're told."

He loosed his grip, and the room, the house, was suddenly empty.

II.

Guerry carried his bed down into the basement. He also brought the refrigerator, couch, and TV, and did his living in the dark dampness. The disability checks came in, and the house, of course, was willed to him. He soon discovered Chinese and Italian delivery and took to drinking beers while watching reality programs and the incessant updates of war.

On these basement nights, a couple beers in him, Guerry's big hands would itch and ache. He held them up to his face, fisting and unfisting them slowly. He listened to his superfluous bones creak like rusty door hinges.

When he woke mornings, he found chunks of the cement wall crumbled on the blankets, fist-sized imprints the culprit.

One morning, Guerry heard Mama calling, and it brought him out of the basement and up to the second floor to her bedroom. The sun coming through the window reflected the clouds of dust. He went into her closet and pulled out an armful of her clothes, hugging and sniffing, soaking them with snot and tears. While doing this, he looked out of the window and noticed an old white man digging out a rectangular plot in the backyard next door. Despite his age, he worked the shovel hard; rings of sweat darkened his back and under his thin arms. The man worked ceaselessly, but with slow progress. The man's wife came out with a glass of iced water. He drank it and put the perspiring glass to his face and neck. The man worked for another half-hour, then went inside. Guerry remained at the window, staring at the black plot of upturned earth.

Guerry paced the basement that evening, flexing his hands, waiting for late night to come. His heart fluttered like the night-before-Christmas. When it was well past midnight, he climbed the stairs and went out the back door into the night. Crickets and the faraway turnpike were the only sounds in the neighborhood. He moved carefully across the backyard, squeezed through the hedges, and stood in the quiet space of the neighbor's lawn, looking at the unfinished garden. His shoulders twitched down to his fingers. He crouched, crawled on all fours to the soil, and put his hands in the cool, damp dirt. He inhaled the rich smell, sucking his lip to keep from drooling. His hands had already begun to work on their own. They knew how to shape themselves into shovels and dig deep. He began minding the noise, but once his body tasted the work, he couldn't contain himself. He dug faster and harder, clearing a larger plot than the old man had marked.

A light from the house froze Guerry in his hunched-over pose. The old man said something to his wife, and his silhouette broke the yellow square. Guerry scrambled off the lawn, through the hedges, and back into his house. He was frightened but exhilarated. His body stank with sweat, hands nicked with cuts, arms and chest caked with dirt.

Guerry revisited the neighbor's yard the next night. This time, he used his thick hands as spades, and simply drew a clean line in the earth with its heel. He had watched the old man toss aside the chunks of grass, so Guerry did the same. Once again, Guerry was interrupted by a light from the upstairs window. On the third night, Guerry didn't have a chance to begin.

"Who are you?" he heard from the shadows of the back porch, then saw the figure of the old man. Guerry was too terrified to move. "You're in no trouble," the old man continued, "unless of course you're up to no good, and then I have a gun, and I'll use it, by God."

The old man was pointing something at him.

Guerry found words and choked them out. "I don't mean any trouble. I was just…" Guerry finally discovered he didn't know what he was doing. He had never attempted to articulate it. "I just wanted to work." It was as close to the truth as he could get.

A light came on, and the old man stepped forward. The gun he claimed to have was an unhinged stapler.

"Don?" the old woman said from inside the house.

"It's okay, Cindy," he called over his shoulder. "You can go on back to bed." Guerry was still crouched, motionless.

"Come on up here, into the light."

The old man was holding out his hand for a shake.

"My hands," Guerry tried to explain.

"Jesus, Mary, and Jo, looky the size of those things." He wasn't mocking. The old man still took his hand, and Guerry was as gentle as he could be. "You must be Miss Johns's boy. Sure sorry for the loss."

"Thank you."

"I'm Donald. Good to know you." The old man's kindness warmed Guerry in the cool night. "I want to thank you for your help, Guerry. But please quit coming in the middle of the night and scaring the bejeezus out of my wife."

"Sorry."

"How 'bout you come by tomorrow morning. You and I can work the garden together. It'll be nice to have some company."

They shook hands again, and again the old man marveled at Guerry's enormity.

"You'll have to excuse me," the old man said. "I heard talk of your arms, seen you around, but I've never seen'm up close."

"S'okay."

The two men worked side-by-side in the crisp spring morning. Guerry dug around the earth for rocks and flung them into the wheelbarrow while Mr. Don worked the hoe. They found a rhythm, grunting and tossing and chopping and maneuvering around each other. When they got to the thick roots of a large nearby maple, Guerry took hold, dug his sneakers in, and yanked with his entire body. The massive tree trembled. "Whoa, Guerry!" Mr. Don intervened. "We don't want to go about it that way."

Miss Cindy came out with drinks, and the two men sat on the back porch admiring their work. Guerry kept the tools nearby to caress their worn wooden handles.

"Those're good tools," Mr. Don said. "Belonged to my father, close to 100 years old."

Guerry gripped their handles in each hand, nodding.

"He was a farmer 'round here, grew tomatoes all his life. I tried to keep it going for a while, but this is no era for farming." He sighed. "No, I had to find me a shirt-and-tie job, but this is where I feel at home, right here." Mr. Don put his hand on Guerry's bulging shoulder. "The world don't need strength these days…it's just a bunch of people sitting on their asses working at computers." He spit and rubbed the back of his neck. "I don't know, Guerry. I don't know about where we're headed, if it's the natural progression of things or the path to destruction."

Guerry rubbed his hair, the old man's words bright as stars. A squadron of fighter jets roared overhead, slashing the sky with a rattling scream.

"But we got this backyard, here," Mr. Don perked.

By mid-October, Guerry and Mr. Don were bundled-up and reshingling the roof. From that height, the autumnal sunlit trees resembled clouds of fire. Many in the neighborhood had their fireplaces going and, from the rooftop, they could smell it, and they talked about the smell.

"Tonight we'll get the fireplace going, Guerry. Nothing better than a roaring fire on a cold night. In fact, we might could clean this out later today." Mr. Don stood up to inspect the chimney, and his feet fumbled. At first, he regained his footing and smiled at Guerry, saying "That was close," then his face deadened, he snatched his chest, and Guerry thought he'd been shot by a sniper. His legs wobbled, and before Guerry could even move, Mr. Don was off the roof.

All afternoon, Guerry sat on the house, looking at the smoke coming from the chimneys and the fiery leaves. His memory was stained with the sounds of Mr. Don's body smacking on the redone patio, Miss Cindy's yelping, hiccupping calls. The sirens. Guerry could not remove himself from the roof, not even when the sky faded from blue to purple to black, then sparkled stars.

III.

Miss Cindy knocked at the front door. She had been doing it all week, but Guerry wasn't going to answer. Moving trucks and family coming indicated she was leaving. She couldn't stay in the house without Mr. Don there. Guerry understood that. Miss Cindy hollered at the front door, her words trickling down into his hole: "I'm leaving the tool shed and all of Donald's tools. I don't want them. Take them, Guerry. Put them to use. Quit hiding in that house; you did nothing wrong."

Guerry went next door that night, the old folks' house quiet as death. He lifted the tool shed clean off the ground and carried it on his back into his yard. He took a hatchet and a rawhide hammer down into the basement and slept with them in bed, dreaming of the project he had planned for his own yard the next day.

Snow fell all that night; the slits of the basement windows were cotton-stuffed with it. Outside, a foot of slush covered the ground. Guerry stuck his arm down in the snow to feel out the earth. It was frozen solid. This wasn't weather for work and, for the next few days, Guerry paced the basement like a wild animal, seething and spitting, his arms screaming. The cement walls showcased fist-sized depressions. Tears sprayed from his eyes, and he bounced around the basement. Roaring and cussing and flailing, a snap happened in his chest. He bounded for the wall and let loose a barrage of punches. Flakes, then hunks, of cement flurried at the fantastic speed of his jackhammer arms, and he didn't quit until his fists landed in soft, steamy dirt. The world stopped spinning, and Guerry paused to examine the destruction: a cross-section of earth—worms and roots and vermin-tunnels veining through the black soil.

He reached out and sunk his hands in and scooped dirt onto his feet. A smile pulled his lips. He dragged out a hefty mound, then another, until there was space enough for him. Guerry crawled into the earth, shaped his hands like shovels, and began to tunnel with the ease of a swimmer cutting water. The soil was cold on his numbing fingertips, the rich coffee-and-metal aroma intense. Grit got into his mouth and eyeballs; pebbles penetrated his ears; clay like cold oatmeal slithered down his shirt and pants. These did not slow him. As he tunneled, he felt the pressure of the earth on his shoulders, not squeezing but vibrating. It was alive—the earth had a pulse, or it was his throbbing heart shuddering the ground.

Tunneling under the neighborhood, he came across water pipes and septic tanks and the cement walls of basements, around or under which he maneuvered. He knew he was moving out of the residential area when his earth-cutting hands collided with animal bones and, maybe, yes, an entire human skeleton. Then he encountered an underground museum of artifacts: pottery, mason jars, kettles and skillets, then arrow heads, musket balls, rifles and knives. When he came to the tools, the earth quivered his excitement. Unsure of their names, he found a stash of items that married iron and wood., pieces big and small with clamps and rings and joints and swivels. Guerry excavated an armful and shimmied homeward, the tools clattering along the way. After nearly an hour, his lungs burning for real air, he saw the orange light of the basement. He crawled out of the hole, and the artifacts clamored on the cement floor. Guerry sucked at the air, looking down at his hands and body coated with dirt.

Guerry took the tools with him into the shower. Once cleaned, the equipments' functions remained mysterious, but their parts—leavers, clamps, and blades—seemed familiar. Like Mr. Don's tools, Guerry simply liked the feel of these instruments in his hands.

That night, Guerry bundled up against the icy draft. He stared into the gaping hole, saw into it the natives and pioneers, the soldiers and farmers, the ghosts that the earth seemed to inhale and exhale like smoke.

Guerry tunneled in a different direction. Perhaps he had burrowed deeper than yesterday or ventured into denser ground, but his lungs burned for lack of air. At first, he kept backtracking to catch his breath but found he was making no progress. He decided to tunnel a diagonal route up to the surface to get a drink of air, careful not to crash through someone's floorboards. After a few days of tunneling, he became strategic with these airholes, pocking the surface every hundred yards in each direction, always mindful of where he poked his head.

He also had holes furtively placed near the dumpsters of banks and at the edge of parking lots of corporations. Sometimes, when Guerry would ascend to get a sip of air, he would take a break from his tunneling to watch the shirt- and-tie people as they went in or came out of office buildings. Some seemed born for the job, marching to and from their cars, talking emphatically at devices attached to their ears. Others moved slowly, clumsily, their briefcases or cell phones as incongruous to them as a dog wearing a sweater.

Guerry spent his non-burrowing time cleaning and restoring the found objects using oils and rags from Mr. Don's shed. His basement became a museum of tools, some of which he could name. Of the smaller category: hammers, spades, hoes, shovels, pick-axes; the larger, the ones that took longer to wrench free from the earth and drag back to the basement: steal plows, harnesses, scythes, wagon wheels. Guerry encountered a few objects deep in the stuffy trenches of the world that came with a shivery, nightmarish vibe: a whip, a bit, rusty chains and shackles. They jolted Guerry when touched, and he left them buried and scurried from their curse.

To organize all of these relics, Guerry built shelves into the walls, transforming the basement into an extension of Mr. Don's shed. He organized the tools by their function, calling on Mr. Don's method for help. The carpentry tools were on one shelf, the garden ones on another, and the very large things leaned on the walls. His bed was relegated to the center of the basement. He left the TV on so he could listen for it while underground to make his way back home and for background noise while polishing tools. The news was the only thing broadcast anymore. The president was shot in the kneecap. Iran had a nuclear bomb, it was confirmed. The stock market crashed, again.

It was the local news, however, that caused Guerry to quit flaking rust from a scythe and watch. A news helicopter captured an aerial shot of a nearby town that Guerry recognized as a place he often poked his head for air. Frighteningly unrecognizable, however, was the gaping depression in the ground, like a sunken cake. The Stop n Shop and liquor store, homes and office buildings, were all angling precariously. A portion of the nearby highway was closed off since the bridges were cracking. The frenzied newscaster said people were urged to evacuate the town, that nobody was hurt, but that buildings and infrastructure could collapse at any moment. Nobody knew what was going on.

Guerry spent the rest of the evening blocking up the tunnel that led out of his basement, then attempting to patch up his wall. The snow had turned to rain. Spring was coming; the earth was thawing. In his mind, Guerry mapped out the maze he had tunneled underground, and it was a webby, intricate one. Of course the ground would collapse. He paced the floor, dizzy with embarrassment and regret, apologizing aloud to Mama and the world. Then he sat down and followed further developments through his thick fingers.

The helicopter views revealed the cinematic carnage. Every day, the sinking earth swallowed another town. The cities began crumbling, rendered to heaps of glass and cement. The cameras often aimed at the periphery of the destruction, where a cliff-like wall nearly a quarter-mile high dramatized the sunken ground. Luckily, the sinking happened gradually enough to evacuate people. Helicopters from all over the country swooped in on New Jersey to carry people to higher ground. Miraculously, no one was killed, though some were injured. There were interviews of the rescued wrapped in blankets, dusty and wide-eyed, attempting to offer insightful explanation, coming up speechless. By May, the coverage showed a gutted, overturned region extending for almost a fifty mile radius of Guerry's home. It looked as though a giant glacier had scoured the earth.

They were saying it was the work of terrorists who, the FBI theorized, had planted little bombs deep underground. Others, expert geologists, argued for previously unknown tectonics gone berserk. Religious leaders said to get your soul right with God; this is the beginning of the end. Celebrities were planning a benefit to raise money for the thousands of displaced. The government promised tax breaks, asked for patience in finding jobs and homes in this economy. For now, the sunken region of New Jersey was deemed uninhabitable—there were no plans or money to rebuild, no time or manpower.

The final images of this news story, before coverage of the War took over once more, were of those who refused to leave the area. The helicopter cameras zoomed in on tiny figures scavenging the rubble, pockets of people gathered here and there, small fires marking their settlements.

IV.

The tribes of settlers had gotten word from various other lone scavengers who claimed to have seen him. Two months had gone by since the Great Collapse, and every crumbled home and grocery store had been picked clean. They needed to find other means of survival, though no one wanted to return to civilization. That much they knew. Old and young, men and women, black, white, Hispanic, Indian, Asian, this multitude of a hundred wore the costumes of their former selves—teachers, bankers, construction workers, landscapers, squatters—though these clothes, now tattered and soiled, had become uniform. Needing food and purpose, the tribes banded together to seek him out.

After two days of searching, they climbed the rubble of a shopping mall on the crest of a summit for vantage. *There he is!* Below, a man was blasting the remains of a cement abutment with a sledgehammer, leveling the formidable structure in three astounding blows. They could almost hear his hammer's whistle as it cut the air. A force of tireless, machine-like movement, he hoisted the massive chunks of cement and hurled them into a pile. He had cleared a plot of land the size of a football field—dark, moist soil with deep, clean rows running longwise. What they said about his arms was true.

Giddy, the group waved and called to him. He shielded the sun with his enormous hand and waved back. They made their way down the summit chattering and chuckling. He was just a young man, quiet but friendly. His name was Guerry Johns. He wasn't sure what he was doing, but *'course you can help. There's a mess of tools*, he said, pointing to a shed and an adjoining structure that resembled a displaced basement. The people went eagerly to the shelves where everything was organized. They took up the tools that called to them, squeezed their handles, quizzed their weight. Then, eagerly, they sought out the job that matched their instrument. Alongside Guerry Johns, they began to cut, clear, plant, and rebuild.

EXCERPTS FROM MIKALA A. PRICE'S THE NEW WHITE HOOD: RACIST VIGILANTISM FROM THE KKK TO THE PRINCE CITY RAT

Mikala Althea Price is a Board of Governors Distinguished Professor of Political Science at New Ark University, an official Prince City Historian, and the author of numerous books on race, politics, and history, including *Politics of the Urban Plantation* and *Prince City Race Riots, 1967-1971*.

> *I recognize no power above the people. Under our Constitution the people are the sovereign authority. And when the courts, the agents, fail to carry out the law the authority is relegated back to the people, who gave it.*
> —William Parkerson

Introduction.

On a warm July Fourth night, after the fireworks have burnt out and the grills have cooled off, a young man is returning from his girlfriend's apartment. We can't know for sure, but maybe he's singing to himself in his new-love excitement; maybe he's even skipping. He has a lot to skip about: he has graduated high school, something his brothers didn't do, and he has a scholarship to attend New Ark University, the first in his family to go to college. What the media has told us is that he's smoking a blunt and carrying a quarter-ounce bag of weed, both facts, yes, but relevant?

Sometime between his girlfriend's place and his own, the infamous vigilante, aptly named the Rat, murdered this young man. There are no witnesses to the crime, no security cameras to capture the details and, worse, no investigation executed by the Prince City Police Department. Instead, the newspapers printed a tiny story, the extent of which was this: the Rat takes down another drug dealer. The young man's name was Brandon Lewis.

American history is bloody with the story of vigilantes who, with the silent nod of authorities, have targeted people of color. From the Know- Nothing Vigilance Committee, the Ku Klux Klan, and the White Citizens' Councils of the past, to the Minutemen militias, the Patriot Movement, and the citizens' patrols and neighborhood watches of the present, the Rat, who, since the late '80s, is responsible for the deaths of close to a thousand Prince City residents of color, is only the most recent example. While the Rat hides behind a black hockey-style airsoft mask, we should see the guise for what it really is: a white hood, for he is carrying out the same racial crimes in the name of justice as the Klan and other white supremacist groups before him. [...]

I. Clean Streets

In 1981, President Ronald Reagan declared a war on drugs, which precipitated the mass incarceration of the African American. The Rat declared his own war on drugs, though because he hides behind a mask, we are uncertain of his motives. Regardless, he is not bound by law, so the Rat's war is literal: he executes the dealers, maims the users and, again, the PCPD allows it. Why wouldn't they? The Rat is making their jobs, and the courts', easier. The media and the public allow it. Why wouldn't they? Drugs are an indefensible crime in their eyes, something they see as a plague in the African American community. By rooting for the Rat, their empathy swells.

Walking down Broad Street in Prince City on any given day, one will undoubtedly encounter the following: people of color with limps, facial burns, deep scars, wheelchairs or crutches, missing fingers, hands, arms, and legs; numerous storefronts, row houses, and churches blackened by fire, riddled with bullets, or rendered to rubble; residents forced to panhandle, to scavenge dumpsters for food, to sleep in doorways and on sidewalks in the shattered glass from those storefront windows. This is what the war on drugs looks like. This is what victory looks like.

The economy of the hood, however, is complicated and rarely discussed in textbooks or the college classroom. When a race has been historically sub-jugated—literally enslaved, and figuratively enslaved by Jim Crow laws, and then enslaved anew by drug laws and mass incarceration—African Americans' opportunities for employment are few and far between. They may have boots, but they have no bootstraps. The types of jobs that they can get without a college or high school diploma are not only limited but barely offer a livable wage. Couple this with the current administration's budget that drastically and cruelly cuts welfare and food-stamp funding, and you only begin to understand their level of desperation. Many resort to a reliable source of income: hustling, dealing, and prostitution. These are their bootstraps, for better or worse.

Yes, this is a dangerous way of life. Yes, this very often breeds gangs and street violence. Yes, this introduces addiction that eventually takes too many lives; but when this alternative source of income is yanked out from underneath their feet *without a viable alternative*, we're replacing death-by-gun and drugs with starvation and suicide. The Rat's methods are just another form of lynching; instead of the strange fruit swinging from Southern trees, we have mangled meat staining Northern streets.

It should be clear, then, that the Rat is not "cleaning up the streets," and the media (not to mention the PCPD) should be excoriated for pitching it as such. [...]

II. First Mask, White Hood

October 22, 1868. It's a windy night in Arkansas, and Republican Con-gressman Henry J. Muntz is on his way to Indian Bay where presidential nom-inee Ulysses S. Grant is holding a campaign event. The election is tomorrow, and Muntz has been campaigning tirelessly for Grant and the ideals of the Republican Party, primarily voting rights for newly-freed African Americans.

Five miles from his destination, Muntz's horse steps into a divot where its hoof gets caught in the root of a shagbark hickory. The horse's leg snaps at the knee. It collapses, and Muntz is tossed onto the path.

The eyes roll back into the horse's head as it kicks and thrashes. Muntz is in a panic. He's already late for the event, and he's been honored with introducing Mr. Grant, for whom he has an immense fondness. The horse, however, is suffering, and Muntz has no sidearm to put it out of its misery. He is torn about whether to continue down the path to hitch a ride to Indian

Bay or to find some creative means of killing the horse. Then, two riders gallop onto the scene, relieving him of the decision. They are wearing conical masks of loose burlap with scarlet stripes, each shouldering an Enfield rifle.

"You Muntz?" one of them barks.

Muntz doesn't respond, for he sees something folded over the rump of one of the horses.

"You that carpetbagger who been talkin 'bout freedom for the negro?" Muntz's wounded horse twists its head to see the masked men. Suddenly, the horse's head explodes, and Muntz's frock is splattered with bone and brain and blood.

"You ready to talk?"

"Yes," Muntz says. "Yes, I am he."

The masked riders sit erect and swell their chests. The first says, "We are the soldiers of the white man's government, vigilantes for the reenfranchisement and emancipation of the white men of the South."

At this point, the second rider reaches behind and pulls the lump off the horse. It is a man, a black man, his throat slit both horizontally and vertically. Muntz has yet to move since the riders arrived.

"You know this man?" the first rider asks but does not wait for a response. "Chief clerk of the Little Rock post office. A goddamn savage monkey holding a position of government."

Muntz does know him, has met and worked with him on numerous occasions. Jonathan Carter Pearce was his name, a good and brave man. One of the thousands of black leaders murdered during the 1868 election season, he was slain in the name of vigilante justice.

Henry Muntz would also die that October night. He and Pearce would be strung up together, hanging side-by-side from a noose over the path to Indian Bay.

The next day, U. S. Grant would be elected President despite the terrorizing efforts to suppress the vote. However, across the South, the proliferation of white supremacist vigilante groups—such as the White League, the Red Shirts, and the Knights of the White Camelia—was just beginning. [...]

III. The Ratist

No one knows more about the Rat's criminal exploits than renowned graffiti artist and Prince City native, Marcel Evans (a.k.a. The Ratist, a clever anagram of Artist), who made a career out of trolling the masked vigilante with his clever, socially-conscious stencils, all depicting rats in some form. My own guided tours of Prince City's historical landmarks now include the Ratist's work, for, like any good historian, he has faithfully documented many of the Rat's significant actions and, like any good artist, he has transformed the destruction into something meaningful.

Take, for instance, the Coe House on Shabazz Boulevard, built in 1899 for leather tycoon Arthur Coe and his family. By 1987, the magnificent house had fallen into disrepair, and the city could not afford to restore it. It was taken over by squatters, the notorious West Ward Crew. In 1991, the St. James Church transformed it into a food bank, serving over 100 residents and families a day. Until the Rat destroyed the house one year later. Allegedly (everything is alleged with the masked vigilante since the PCPD refuses to investigate his crimes), the food bank was a cover for dealing heroin and guns by the West Ward Crew, though this claim cannot be substantiated. What we know is that the historic Coe House and St. James Food Bank were the focus of a shoot-out that resulted in a fire that turned the century- old building into a blackened, gutted, and partially-razed reminder of the Rat's racial profiling.

Drawing attention to the injustice leveled here, the Ratist created a poignant piece on the building's charred facade (photos below). The nearly six-foot stencil was significant for numerous reasons. It was the first known public protest of the Rat's vigilantism, which, prior to this, had been celebrated by the media and the white folks who commuted to Prince City for work. Second, the stencil situated the Rat into a historical context that elegantly and vividly criticized his actions in a way that empowered the local African American community.

[photo]
Historic Coe House, 1901.

[photo]
Coe House/St. James Food Bank still smoldering one day after the Rat leveled it for yet unknown reasons, 1992.

[photo]
Ratist stencil no. 1, Rat w Hood on Horse w Torch, Coe House, 1992.

At one time, there were rumors from some in the black community that the Ratist was the Rat. The neighborhood barber shops, diners, and churches were abuzz with colorful theories of how the Ratist, who in those days had not revealed his identity, seemed to know before the authorities or anyone else where the Rat had struck. When, in 2004, the *Ledger's* Arts & Culture section ran a cover story about the Ratist, these theories were quickly abated. It was a photo of Marcel posing beside the six-foot stencil on Coe House, exposing his diminutive stature, that hushed the rumors.

However, new rumors soon took hold. This time, the Rat and Ratist were working together, planning the initial strike to correlate with the intended graffiti as a kind of performance art. Typically good-natured and soft-spoken, Marcel took great offence to these rumors, for it was as obvious to him as it was to me that the Rat was targeting his community. His next piece, my personal favorite, sought to dispel this theory:

[photo]
The Ratist stencil/tag no. 13, Rat impaled by paint brush and strangled by Marcel's tag, Hahne's building, 2004.

Ironically, it was Marcel's efforts to disprove that he was the Rat that garnered national attention, blazing his celebrity in the art and hip-hop world, albeit briefly. From 2005-2009, he and his work were recognized by the likes of Banksy, Jay-Z, and Brad Pitt; he was awarded a Guggenheim fellowship and had his first (and only) one-person show at the New Ark Museum. However, his growing fame brought out vandals and thieves targeting his street art. At least three of his stencils were stolen completely when the perpetrators cut the walls they were painted on and hauled them away. A few more of his pieces were vandalized with random tags. Eventually, Marcel recruited the local gangs to help protect his work. It is still unclear (to me) whether he paid them, whether the soldiers simply did their hometown celebrity a favor, or whether there was some other arrangement. Regardless, his relationship with the gangs was his undoing.

When a curator from the MoMA ventured into Prince City to take photos of the Ratist's work, she was gunned down, presumably by the fiercely loyal and territorial West Ward Crew. The art world cut all ties with the Ratist after that; even the hip-hop community recognized the indefensibility of the murder and turned their backs on him. Marcel refuses to speak about this and, for at least three years, even while the Rat continued to terrorize the streets, the Ratist's spray paint never touched a wall. Those closest to him, his mother and his girlfriend, tell me that during those years, he remained in his bedroom all day, reading comics and playing video games and occasionally watching cartoons with his four-year-old niece.

Incidentally, it was the Rat who compelled him out of seclusion and back to work. [...]

[photo]
Ratist stencil no. 2, Rat Trampling Children, Hotel Divine, 1994.

[photo]
The Ratist stencil no. 7, Intoxicated Rat, Former Pabst Brewery, 1998.

[photo]
Ratist stencil no. 11, Rat Scurrying into Gutter, sidewalk on Halsey Street, 2003.

[photo]
Ratist mixed media no. 21, Rat illumined with 'GO HOME!,' East Ward, 2014.

IV. Mobs without Masks

"We want the Dagoes! We Want the Dagoes!" they chant outside the Parish Prison, New Orleans as the leaders of the mob bash at the door with a battering ram.

Inside the prison, the petrified Italian prisoners scramble to hide under their bunks or in dark corners, but options are slim in a cell. Cowering and praying, they hear the prison doors crash and the mob's stampede through the corridors—their growls and threats, their clubs and rifle stocks clanging on the bars, echoing in the stony walls. One prisoner, Salvatore Februzzio from Sicily, snatches a handful of flour from the kitchen and douses his face with it, hoping to cover his olive complexion. But as he hides in the stuffy pantry, he can't control the sweat that dribbles down his forehead, gumming up the flour.

One of the largest mass lynchings in America's history was not of African Americans, but of Southern Italian immigrants. Modern readers may have forgotten, or were never aware, that at the turn of the twentieth century, Italians, especially Sicilians, were not considered white, but rather "Dagoes" of Mediterranean heritage—the "swarthy link" between the white and black races whom the mayor of New Orleans publically vilified as "idle, vicious, worthless… [and] filthy." This nativism, like most bigotry, had as much to do with skin color as class: the Italian immigrants came in droves to this country after the Civil War, in part to replace the slaves working the fields. Incidentally, the focus on Sicilians as Other is a supreme irony, especially to Prince City historians, since the most racist backlash during the '67 riots came from Italian Americans, some of whom formed their own vigilante groups that targeted African Americans.[1] [...]

It all started with a murder. On a windy night in October of 1890, the police chief of New Orleans, David Hennessy, was gunned down in the streets on his way home from work. With his dying breath, he allegedly uttered the word "Dagoes." At that, hardly an investigation was necessary. The only question was how many of the city's Italian immigrants should be rounded up and arrested. Not twenty-four hours after Hennessy's death, and at the mayor's insistence, 249 Italians were taken in for questioning, 45 were arrested, and 19 were ultimately charged.

When many of the suspects were acquitted due to a lack of evidence and a mistrial was declared for others, a mob of roughly 150 whites gathered outside of the prison where the Italians were ordered to return. The organizers of the mob called themselves the Committee on Safety. They wore no masks. In times of extreme nativism, masks are not necessary when the targets are hated by the populous. In fact, the Committee was comprised of well-known and recognizable white members of New Orleans: one would become governor of Louisiana and another, mayor; others were businessmen, attorneys, and newspaper editors. Their reputations would remain untarnished even after they participated, identities on full display, in the public murder of eleven innocent men.

Salvatore can hear the screams of his friends. The gunshots sound like canonfire, but it's the sound of the clubbing that makes him vomit on his

---

1   The infamous Anthony Imperiale formed the North Ward First Aid Squad, an armed, nighttime patrol group comprised of Italian-Americans that baited and antagonized blacks from 1967-1969.

shoes, the bashing of skull yielding to pulp. All he can think of are the watermelons falling from a cart and crashing on the street back home. He topples forward, weeping, exposing himself to the main corridor. There, he sees the white men dragging Emmanuele and Antonio, old friends from his village back home, toward the exit.

The angry multitude outside the prison are hungry for justice, too. They must be fed. Feed them a hardworking fruit vendor and another who is mentally ill, both of whom are dragged from the prison by their collars, both of whom had just hours before been acquitted. One is strung up on a lamppost, the other on a tree. Both are riddled with bullets by the hungry mob. Both are left hanging in the streets for hours as their blood puddles at their feet.

Not a single individual of the lynch mob was indicted after the murder of the eleven Sicilians. The grand jury claimed that it was impossible to identify anyone involved— impossible to name well-known men who wore no masks.

Three decades later, in Phillips County, Arkansas, another mass lynching led by a vigilante mob occured. [...]

V. The Arc of Policing Bends towards Injustice

The earliest record we have of the Rat's vigilantism appears in the *Ledger* in October of 1985. The headline reads, "Mysterious Man Takes Down Heads of DeLuccio Crime Family." It goes on to say, "This alleged vigilante single-handedly dismembered the most powerful and long-standing mafia family in New Jersey. The only witness is Nero 'The Greek' himself, who, before expiring from his wounds, told authorities that 'a rat' was to blame."

Initially, PCPD took this to mean that a mafia insider was the vigilante, but further investigation found that there were no such informants. Drawing on a handful of eye witnesses throughout the decades, it is possible that the Rat earned his rodent appellation from his black and brown tactical gear and black mask, his penchant for emerging from or retreating into sewers and manholes, and his filthy exterior and garbagey stench. Unlike characters from comic books, the Rat has no self-identifying symbols stitched into his uniform (and certainly no tights or cape). This is significant, to me at least, that he has no delusions of grandeur: he doesn't seem to want to be identified or named. Make no mistake, this is not a praiseworthy character trait. If anything, it is cowardly, not to mention criminal, to hide behind a mask. At the very least, the Rat is an appropriate nomenclature.

Regardless, the Rat soon became a local hero and was heralded by the newspapers for exacting the kind of swift justice that the local and federal authorities were incapable of. To an extent, I agree with this exaltation: the DeLuccios ran a sex trafficking ring out of the North Ward with girls as young as twelve, and they were one of the largest suppliers of crack, which they dealt almost exclusively in the black neighborhoods. Had the Rat ended his vigilantism with the fall of the DeLuccios, I might be writing an entirely different book. Sadly, this was not the case. He moved on to the black neighborhoods of the West Ward, perhaps going after the Bloods and the West Ward Crew, who at the time had a small presence in the neighborhoods. This is where the Rat's misunderstanding of the black community proved disastrous.

After the Rat dismantled the DeLuccios, he most likely assumed that the same tactics could be successful against the the Prince City gangs. However, while the Italian mafia and black street gangs share a few similarities, the understanding of the former does not yield an insight into the latter. The arms of a gang like the West Ward Crew are threaded throughout the community, a community knit so tightly it's nearly impossible to extricate the "bad thread" without unraveling the whole tapestry. For example, an unaffiliated eighth grader could deal marijuana to his classmates for his older brother who may be a prospect. The classmates, the eighth grader, and even the older brother are not part of the gang. They may not be innocent citizens, but they are certainly not murderers, gun-smugglers, or high-level dealers that one may find in a gang. In other words, it is as impossible to go after a black gang without harming residents as it is to drop a bomb on ISIS without killing hundreds of civilians. While the Rat's intentions to go after the gangs seems irreproachable on the surface, the way he executed it—like a human bomb—was deplorable.

The Rat continued to level his violence on the black community for two decades, never relenting. Incidentally, it wasn't until the Rat turned his sites away from the mafia and onto African Americans that the PCPD began to leave him alone.

The Rat's trajectory is a microcosm of America's police force: it begins with good intentions and just results but, inevitably, it bends toward (racial) injustice; that injustice breeds more animosity and distrust from the African American community, which results in more profiling. Ironically, but not paradoxically, the police and the Rat create more crime to give their jobs purpose.

What is not known is how many of these homicides are attributed to the Rat alone, since the PCPD conveniently fail to keep a file on him. However, what is clear is that under his "watch," crime has increased. This is the paradox of vigilantism (and excessive policing) that the media fails to report, and it was the same in the early twentieth century in the areas where the Klan rampaged. It was the same in the Jim Crow South when average white citizens "policed" African Americans by blockading segregated schools and guarding lunch counters, and it was the same when Neo-Nazis held rallies and parades which inevitably incited violence. This paradox is ignored because the alternative would be too shocking for White America, which feels safer with the police protecting them from people of color: less policing equals fewer crimes. [...]

VI. The White Rat of Kentucky

[...] He wears a white hockey mask quartered by a scarlet cross and the same tactical gear as the Prince City Rat—bulletproof vest, elbow and knee pads, tactical boots, knuckle gloves—but his are painted all-white. He carries a white shield bearing a black iron cross with a white rat in its center. This is the self-proclaimed White Rat.

The White Rat made his first appearance during a Black Lives Matter protest in Louisville, two weeks after the shooting of Michael Brown in Ferguson, Missouri. It was uneventful but unnerving nonetheless. He weaved through the crowd, shouting in German like a madman. The protesters taunted him, but there were no physical altercations. The Louisville police later commented that they had kept an eye on him the entire night and decided that he posed no threat.

That changed two nights later.

Monday, August 18, 2014, 10:00 p.m. Three male students from the University of Louisville are walking back to their dorms from the McDonald's just off campus. They have completed their first day of classes as sophomores. They are optimistic, energized. They are singing and laughing. One of the young men, Albert Patterson, is wearing a Black Lives Matter T-shirt. Apparently, that is their undoing.

The White Rat fires twenty rounds into their backs with an AR-15 semiautomatic rifle, killing all three on site. He then removes Mr. Patterson's bloody shirt, drapes it over his rifle like a flag, and runs through campus, chanting, "white heritage matters." This goes on for fifteen minutes before police arrive and shoot him dead.

The identity of this vigilante does not deserve to be repeated. Suffice it to say, when authorities looked into his social media presence, they found numerous postings on his Facebook page praising the Rat of Prince City for having the courage to stand up. [...]

VII. The Perfect Breeding Ground

Since the Rat's arrival in 1985, there have been numerous copycat vigilantes across the country. The White Rat is the most well known, but others include The Utopian from Greensboro, North Carolina, Beta X from Southern Indiana, and the citizens patrol group who go by Suck Life out of Tampa, Florida, to name a few. However, none have been nearly as successful as Prince City's own Rat, who, despite numerous investigations, manhunts, and bounties, has astonishingly evaded capture. How is this possible? Navy Seals were able to hunt down Osama bin Laden in the labyrinthine terrain of Pakistan but, for thirty years, we know as little about the Rat and his whereabouts as we did after his first appearance in Prince City.

Over the years, there have been a few attempts to investigate the infamous vigilante, all of which had little-to-no effect. *Time Magazine*, in its profile from October 1997, weighed in on the Rat's probable training as a Navy Seal, Green Beret, Army Ranger, or some other top-secret special ops agent. They managed to get a statement from a mid-level staff member at the Pentagon about the Rat, the one and only acknowledgement of the vigilante from the federal government: "If such an individual exists, he should be considered extremely dangerous. But rest assured; if he's one of ours, he will be found."[2]

In 2005, the NAACP secretly hired a team of private investigators to track down the Rat. They located someone of interest and convinced the PCPD to bring the individual in for questioning. He fit the profile—large, ex-military, a recluse—but it turned out he was too mentally unstable to be capable of the Rat's feats. Conservative media exploited the NAACP's failed effort, blowing it up to a colossal waste of resources and a misguided attempt to racialize an issue for their own fame.

---

2   When I tried to locate this Pentagon employee, Ronin Sparks, there were virtually no records that I could find of him. The Pentagon could not be reached for comment, and *Time* simply said it "stands by [its] reporting."

The lack of information about the Rat has fueled the internet's imagination. On countless blogs and message boards, theories are as wild and imaginative as any fantasy or sci-fi novel. Here are just a few:

- The Rat is Russian KGB charged with destabilizing American cities;
- The Rat is a government-trained operative who in the late '80s introduced crack to the city's underprivileged to turn it into a criminal wasteland;
- The Rat is a subhuman creature who's been living in the sewers for centuries; (there is a 19th Cent. photo "of him" that these theorists provide as evidence)

Skill alone doesn't account for how the Rat has been able to have his way with the city for a quarter of a century. The other, more elemental and terrible explanation is the unique personality of Prince City: its history, its government, its law enforcement, and the physical layout of the city create the perfect environment for someone like the Rat to thrive. He may have had a good run in Chicago, Detroit, Cleveland, or Baltimore, but only in Prince City with its complicated race history and problematic string of police chiefs could he have run amok for so long.

In my earlier book, *Prince City Riots, 1967-1971*, I discussed the racial tensions that lead to the two-week riot resulting in the deaths of thirty African Americans and two police officers. The fallout from the riots that I wrote about included the demise of Prince City's "inner city" due to middle-class families moving to the suburbs, the increase in poverty and crime, and the increase in tensions between blacks and police that has yet to be resolved. The fourth major consequence of the riots is that it laid the groundwork for someone like the Rat to come into existence. Not only did the inner city neighborhoods become economically vulnerable, which saw a rise in gangs and crime, but the PCPD under the helm of Chief William Shaw became more aggressive in their handling of African Americans in those neighborhoods; they had the support of the media and surrounding residents who saw in the newspapers and on TV the constant portrayal of looting and destruction.[3] The incarceration of African American males in New Jersey grew by 135% in the next thirty years: from 1,400 in 1977 to 18,900 in 2007. (Figure 6.1) This resulted in a rise in violence against the police; in 1995, twenty-seven

---

3   As I wrote in *Prince City Riots*, there were numerous peaceful protests happening on the steps of city hall that were never covered.

officers were murdered in Prince City, the second-most ever recorded in a single American city. (The first was on 9/11/2001 in New York City.)

So when the Rat came on the scene and eventually targeted the inner city, the PCPD, the mayor, the white residents, and the media openly praised the vigilante's aggression. [...]

VIII. The End of Terror

The Ledger coined it "The Summer of Terror." By September of 2015, twenty-two people would be killed, not one of them in the same manner. Among standard shooting, stabbing, and strangulation were more creative and disturbing methods: poisoning, electrocution, dismemberment, immolation— each murder a horror story in itself. The victims would be of all ages, genders, races, and classes, though Hispanics and African Americans would comprise two-thirds of the dead. By the end of June, Prince City would be in a state of emergency with a 9 p.m. curfew. By the end of July, with few leads and fewer suspects, the FBI took over the investigation, and 5,000 National Guard occupied the city. By the end of August, the death count still growing and the FBI and ARNG making no progress, Mayor Higgs held a historic and extraordinary press conference: he made a public plea to the Rat for assistance.

Up until this point, the Rat was never acknowledged by a public official. Every five years or so, the local media outlets would do a new story on him, but interest would fizzle when no new details emerged. Sources close to the PCPD said it was the department's unofficial position not to comment on the Rat. Therefore, even though everyone in Prince City knew of his existence, especially the African American community, the Rat was relegated to myth.

All of that changed on August 21.

There is still much we don't know about the mayor's appeal. For example, in order for him to make such a request, the FBI must have concluded that the Rat was not responsible for the murders. After all, he had to have been a prime suspect (even though his name never came up as such). Secondly, the FBI, the National Guard, and the PCPD must have agreed to give the Rat space, for one could easily imagine using the plea as a kind of trap. While the local police understandably wouldn't want to remove the Rat from their streets, the federal government certainly would, especially if he was ex-military.

All of this is secondary to what I find most crucial, and seemingly problematic, to my thesis, and that is, the Rat came through for Prince City. Less than two weeks after Mayor Higgs's press conference, a man now known as the Terror was discovered bound, gagged, and barely alive on the steps of the municipal courthouse just as the sun was coming up. Strapped to this man, later identified as Brent Hayden, Jr., former PCPD officer-turned-conservative- blogger, was a duffel bag containing all the weapons he used during his violent spree, a notebook filled with disturbing sketches and poetry, and a laptop with a damning browsing history—all the evidence needed to convict the Terror without a shadow of a doubt.[4]

This isn't a clear-cut case of moral rectitude—far from it. The most glaring question is why the Rat waited to help until he was asked, especially given that it took him virtually no time at all to find and turn in the perpetrator. Certainly, he must take some pride in a city that after almost thirty years, must seem like his turf. And yet, he allowed someone else to take over Prince City for the entire summer? The cynical view is that he knew who it was all along and turned his head as innocent victims were killed. The other way of looking at this is more complicated, and at the time of writing this book, still difficult to accept.

Two security cameras captured the Rat bringing the Terror up the courthouse steps and then fleeing. The clip is only a half-minute long, but it reveals so much.

The Rat carrying the Terror up the steps is remarkable in that it shows the Rat's legendary strength. According to the police report, Hayden, Jr., is six feet tall and weighs 195 pounds; in the footage, however, he looks like a straw-stuffed dummy by the way the Rat carries him over his shoulder and flops him down.

His strength is not what interested me, nor is it what stood out to the doctors to whom I showed this footage.

When the Rat releases the Terror, you immediately notice the severe tremor in his hands. The second camera footage conveys this best: the Rat drops the Terror and his duffel bag, and his hands flutter like tortured butterflies. Then you can see the Rat stumble, not once or twice, but four times in the short distance at the bottom of the frame (roughly seven steps). After his second stumble, he appears disoriented; he lifts himself up, turns back toward the courthouse, looks down to the Terror, then resumes his drunken movements down the steps.

---

4   At the time of this writing, jury selection for Hayden, Jr.'s trial has just begun.

Initially, I thought he was inebriated, except that the trembling hands didn't fit. An alcoholic will certainly shake in this way when enduring withdrawal but, of course, that wouldn't fit with the appearance of intoxication. This is when I reached out to the medical community. I took the footage to three different doctors in Prince City, all of whom, independent of one another, confirmed that the Rat is most likely suffering from Chronic traumatic encephalopathy (CTE). This is the same disease from which numerous NFL players and boxers suffer. All three doctors, two of whom are neurologists, explained how CTE could have developed in the Rat's brain over a quarter century after absorbing kicks, punches, and blows to the head with heavy objects; falls and proximity to explosions would add to the trauma, and all of this was endured while wearing nothing more than a plastic mask.

Most interesting is what Dr. Susan Chin told me from her office at St. Michael's. She guessed that the Rat's condition was severe and that he must have been experiencing noticeable symptoms for at least two years—the kind of symptoms that would impair judgement and interfere with physical tasks. She hinted that the Rat couldn't endure these symptoms for much longer without hospitalization and, regardless of treatment, he'd most likely be dead within the year. She said this almost sadly while gazing at the paperwork on her desk.

IX. The Historian's Job

When I returned to my office at New Ark, I began searching our library's database for the most recent reports of the Rat's activity. I couldn't wrap my head around the idea that the Rat would have been physically and mentally impaired for the past two years. My search didn't yield any helpful results. The few sources at the *Ledger* on whom I had previously relied were no longer working, and I don't have to explain what my relationship with the PCPD is like. Running out of options, I called on Marcel Evans, the Ratist.

At this point, recall that he'd been in retirement for five years, and other than a few emails of encouragement, I'd respected his seclusion. I wasn't sure, then, if he would answer his cell or whether he'd resent me as being part of the problem from which he was hiding. Needless to say, I did not expect him to pick up after one ring. It seemed as though he'd been waiting for my call. I hadn't even finished explaining to him what I was looking for when he asked to meet with me.

"When?"

"Tonight. Now. How's now?"

It was 8 p.m., almost sundown, but I agreed.

He told me to meet him at the corner of Clinton Avenue and 11th Street in the East Ward. I know every elbow of the city, but if there's a forgotten part of it, this would be the place. Standing there alone, just a few moments from nightfall, was not a comfort. A rattling on the rooftop across the road caused me to yelp. I'm not ashamed to tell you that I believed the Rat was going to leap from the five-story building in some kind of ambush an unstable Marcel had orchestrated. Instead, it was a cheery Marcel.

"Oh, hey, Professor," he said, waving with a wrench in his hand. "Be down in a second."

He maneuvered something large and rectangular, like a huge flat screen TV or mini billboard. It squeaked as he swivelled it to face me. He then sprayed the surface and wiped it clean with a rag. I've known the Ratist long enough to never question or underestimate him. He's a brilliant artist and social activist. Still, he was leaving me quite literally in the dark. When he finally joined me, breathless and fidgety like a ten-year-old, he told me the story of this street corner and the building we stood next to.

It was luck or coincidence that brought the Ratist to this neighborhood that night almost a year ago. He said he had begun venturing out of his apartment, wandering the neighborhoods late at night, searching for inspiration, and scavenging for materials that might rejuvenate his art. It was then that he spotted a colossal figure in uniform, moaning like a wounded animal. In this very spot, the Rat was on his knees, butting his head on the bricks. Occasionally, he would try to stand. He'd get his knees off the concrete for a few moments but then crash back to the sidewalk. Most disturbingly, he had some kind of taser wand and, every so often, he would press it to his head behind his ear and zap himself. He'd scream out in pain and dry heave, but the jolt would appear to snap him from his misery, at least for a few minutes, until he returned to moaning and sobbing.

According to Marcel, who watched from across the street, the Rat remained in this constant state of slow self-torture for the entire night. At first, Marcel said he thought the Rat had been mortally wounded. However, when the sun began to rise, he seemed to awaken from whatever nightmare he was in. He stood, but not too stable, and fled into what was left of the shadows.

Marcel returned the next night out of curiosity and, sure enough, he found the Rat in the same place, moaning and butting his head. Apparently, he was there again and again. After the fourth consecutive night, moved by an empathy that was and is beyond me, Marcel tossed rocks and empty cans in the Rat's direction to break him out of his reverie and get him gone.

At this point in his story, I interjected.

"Why did you shoo him away? Why not call someone and have him taken in?"

"You know that ain't the code. Besides, I don't want that on me."

"Want what?"

"His capture." Marcel was less interested in this conversation than he was in polishing tiles fastened to the wall. "Whatever they might do to him if he's captured, I don't want on my shoulders."

I pushed back. I explained what he already knows, the long list of the Rat's crimes against our community. I was heated, I'll admit. I may have put my finger in his face and stabbed some accusations at him, which distracted him from the wall.

"I'm trying to get back to anonymity," he explained defensively. "Get back to watching and creating. My paint will get involved, but the day I step in and interfere, I become the watched. That ain't my role."

"But what about—"

"*That ain't my role, Professor.*"

I had much more to say, but he hushed me and told me to watch. He looked over his shoulder to the rooftop. I could now see what he'd been maneuvering: a large mirror. It was catching the light of a streetlamp on the opposite side of the building that was flickering on as the sky darkened. I followed Marcel's gaze from the mirror to the wall right before us. The reflective light illumined hundreds of glass tiles of various sizes and shapes that I hadn't fully noticed until now. It looked like the wall was lit up from the inside. There was a shape, a message, that I couldn't quite appreciate from this close. I took a few steps back.

The rough image of a rat sparkled into view along with these words: GO HOME! The jagged message dazzled in the night, a bright and brilliant display. I understood immediately how this would alarm the Rat, drive him off from the spot that was no longer shrouded in privacy.

Marcel watched the glittery wall art as if he wasn't the one who put it there. He said, "He hasn't been back since."

"It's magnificent," I replied, completely forgetting my anger. Somehow, the beauty of the Ratist's work softened me to the Rat's condition in a way that neither the video footage nor the doctors' diagnoses had.

"What do you make of it?" I asked. "His brain damage. His capturing the Terror?"

Odd-angled pieces of light landed on Marcel's face as he pondered my question. It seemed he was trying to determine if it was worth answering. Finally, he said softly, "He tried to do something good before his end."

"Do you forgive him?" The words were out of my mouth before I fully understood what I was asking.

He smiled, appearing as boyish as he did nearly thirty years ago when we first met. "It ain't the artist's job to forgive. That's for you historians to rassle with." [...]

PROLOGUE.

[...] When I review the now-famous footage of the Rat stumbling down the courthouse steps, I am ashamed for feeling pity. I feel duped for believing that he sacrificed himself for the city. These are the same reluctant emotions I feel when seeing news clips of frail, elderly men with breathing tubes sitting in courtrooms who are finally convicted of some despicable crimes they committed decades earlier, for I only have to walk three blocks to visit my cousin who is wheelchair bound, or my neighbor's son laced with scars, or any number of other citizens who bear the markings of the Rat's excessive and racist force.

The hope I feel, however, is absolute. The Rat will die, and soon, taken by an accumulation of all those people of color who tried to fight back. They did not fail in their defense. Like so many instances in the long war against oppression, the effects are brutally slow, but there will be justice, even if it comes in the form of a brain-addled tyrant stumbling down the steps of justice.

THE BAD THAT CAN HAPPEN THE DAY JESUS ROSE FROM THE DEAD

Bush tore down the middle of Sweet Lane, and I chased him, my knees all bloodied up as I called him Low Down. We sprinted through the peach orchard, my Easter dress raked once by his hands, now again by the blooming branches. I cornered him at Ruin Lake, brown like caramel and Bush's dark shoulders.

"I'll bust you up," I screamed, knocking him over as he was getting a leg out of his trousers. "What Mom gonna say about my dress?"

"She'll call you a clumsy twit for falling all over yourself before church." All gums and crooked teeth, he was down on the dew-grass, the sun glowing him beautiful. It made me hate him even more for leaving tomorrow for juvie. Last week, he had gutted Miss Hinshaw's poodle with a butterfly knife. I didn't see him do it, but that night, he came into my bedroom when I was sleeping. I made space for him, thinking he'd get in bed as he sometimes did, but he handed over the knife instead. It had white tufts of hair stuck to it, the blood sticky like syrup. He said to hide it, so I wrapped the blade in a pair of my underwear and buried it in the back of the drawer. It didn't matter, though, since Miss Hinshaw was witness to the killing, and the police came by the next afternoon. The judge gave him 90 days, starting tomorrow.

From his back, Bush kicked out my legs, and I crashed stupidly. He scrambled into the lake and splashed me.

"Fool," I spat. "You gone to hell."

He took out his noodley penis and peed in the water. He cranked his shoulders backwards and made the pee arch like a fountain. I pretended not to look but looked. Mom was hell-bent on getting Bush's soul right with the Lord. She had been talking about the Lamb of God all Easter weekend and convinced the pastor to baptize his sorry butt before he went away. Now, in only a few hours, Pastor was going to dip Bush's head in pee while we all sang "Angel Band."

Bush jumped like he'd been bit, and he cussed the water. He scurried out and studied the lake.

"What is it?" I got beside him to look. "A gi-normous scorpion, I swear it." "Go on."

Just as I said it, a thick cloud of gold-flecked mud kicked up. When it cleared, there was the coiled tail of a huge lobster-looking thing kicking around just under the surface. It was the size of a dog, not including its horrible red legs and claws. Its tail whipped and snapped, spraying both our shins. Then it crawled deeper into the lake until it disappeared into the depths.

My whole body budded with hives.

"Come on, Sis." Bush was trotting to the old aluminum rowboat upside down in the high grass. "We're going to chase that thing. I want it. I could win something for having it."

He flipped the boat, pushed it into the water, and got in. I stood in the grass with my arms folded.

"There's no way I'm getting in with you."

"Might be others crawling round in the grass," he said, pushing off. "Bush!" I caught up to the boat and climbed in. "God knows I hate you."

The sun shone on his snapping muscles yanking the oars. His body looked different in the light, different than it felt in the dark. I kept my eyes on the thread of his arms because I didn't dare look into the water. I repeated Lamb of God in my head. I thought nothing this bad could happen the day Jesus rose from the dead.

In the middle of the lake, Bush yelped, "Good night!" and pulled in the oars. He was big-eyed looking over the boat, and I couldn't help but to look, too. The lake around us bubbled and spit, and there was a swelling buzz like a million cicadas just under the water. This swarm of whatever-they-were rushed the boat, pecking the sides and belly, the metal pocked like shotgun fire. Bush was frozen, not even breathing. I began to pee myself and bunched the dress between my legs to sponge it.

I scrambled into Bush's lap, pressed my face into his sweaty chest, tasting its metallic saltiness, pleading with his body as I had done on the nights he came into the room when he'd hush me, promise me it was good love. His arms draped me. His heart slammed my temple like God had gotten into him and became frightened by what He saw and was punching to get out. Water coming into the boat licked our ankles. His heart thumped fiercer than when he had claimed to love me, and the water was the same cool of the butterfly knife that still lay hidden in my drawer. My heart suddenly sprouted its tail, which, seeping poison, sought its victim.

I pushed myself from Bush and, lying back on the bottom of the boat, fired both feet smack into his chest. The loud white of his eyes caught the sun as he fell backwards into the lake. I sobbed as I watched the electric swarm bubble around him, his arms waving like mad, his screams going from jagged to gurgle. The peach of his palms were the last things I saw, descending quickly into the dark. As the lake went peaceful once again, I reached over the bow for the water, screaming his name.

ACKNOWLEDGMENTS

First, I would like to thank Kimberly Verhines and the staff at Stephen F. Austin University Press for accepting and working on my manuscript. I would also like to thank Jason Hopkins for designing the cover. These stories have been fifteen years in the making. Some were workshopped by my generous instructors and classmates at Rutgers University-Newark; others were read and critiqued by my wonderful friends, Sam Starnes, Kris Saintsing, Zach Herrmann, my brilliant brother Brian, and my remarkable wife, Megan; all were edited by so many tireless small-press editors who deserve endless praise; a few were even written with my beautiful children, Cameron and Sam, harnessed to my heart in a baby bjorn; and all were written with the unconditiontal support of my mom and dad, and especially my wife.

KEVIN CATALANO is the author of *Where the Sun Shines Out,* a literary thriller published by Skyhorse. Other writing has appeared in places like *Fanzine, PANK, storySouth,* and *Gargoyle Magazine.* He teaches writing at Rutgers University-Newark, and lives in New Jersey with his wife and two children.

CPSIA information can be obtained
at www.ICGtesting.com
Printed in the USA
FSHW012217050320
67842FS

9 781622 883035